# A REASONABLE WORLD

Tor Books by Damon Knight

*A For Anything*
*CV*
*The Observers*

# A REASONABLE WORLD

# DAMON KNIGHT

TOR®

A TOM DOHERTY ASSOCIATES BOOK
NEW YORK

This is a work of fiction. All the characters and events
portrayed in this book are fictitious, and any resemblance
to real people or events is purely coincidental.

A REASONABLE WORLD

A Tor Book
Published by Tom Doherty Associates, Inc.
49 West 24th Street
New York, N.Y. 10010

Library of Congress Cataloging-in-Publication Data

Knight, Damon Francis
    A reasonable world / Damon Knight.
        p.    cm.
    "A Tom Doherty Associates Book."
    ISBN 0-312-85077-8
    I. Title.
    PS3561.N44R4 1991
    813'.54—dc20                                    90-48783
                                                        CIP

Printed in the United States of America

First edition: February 1991

0  9  8  7  6  5  4  3  2  1

In loving memory of
ERIC FRANK RUSSELL
a friend I never knew

# A REASONABLE WORLD

The twentieth century was one of great change and turmoil. The First and Second World Wars claimed 87 million lives, both military and civilian; in the Spanish Civil War and in the Second World War, for the first time in the century, civilian populations were strategically targeted. One hundred thirty-five thousand perished in the fire-bombing of Dresden, 110,000 more in the atomic bombing of Hiroshima and Nagasaki. Mortalities in the nuclear destruction of Tel Aviv–Jaffa totaled 500,000. Counting lesser conflicts in Asia, Africa, the Middle East and Latin America, the death toll was 92 million.

During the same period, the population of the world rose from 1.5 billion to 5 billion. It had been projected to reach 6 billion by the year 2000, but fell short of that mark by reason of the famines, pandemics, and world-wide economic collapse of the late nineties.

Nevertheless, extensive ecological damage had already been done. Acid rain from industrial and automobile emissions had destroyed many of the forests of Europe and North America. The deliberate deforestation of the Mato Grosso had turned that area into a desert; together with acid rain and other deforestation around the globe, this led to extensive changes in global temperature, weather patterns and the oxygen content of the ocean and atmosphere. Many perished in floods, typhoons and hurricanes, or starved as a consequence of flood and drought in unexpected places.

In the last year of the century a new challenge confronted the world: McNulty's Symbiont, named for the physician who discovered it aboard the ocean habitat Sea Venture. It was later determined that MS was a coherent energy system, possibly of extraterrestrial origin, capable of intelligent action and of taking human beings and other animals as hosts. Its influence on human beings was alarming: former hosts exhibited a strong tendency to break their vocational and emotional ties, leading to a crisis for industry and government. As they proliferated through the population, using rats and other small mammals as intermediate hosts, the symbionts began to interdict most acts of violence on the part of human beings.

By the year 2005 the world was in the grip of sweeping change. For the first time in centuries, there was no war or threat of war anywhere in the world. Other changes, at first imperceptible, were altering human society in unprecedented ways.

*The Twenty-first Century*
by A. R. HOWARTH and LYNETTE FORD

*1* Stanley Bliss, Ex–Chief of Operations of the ocean habitat Sea Venture, had been for some years living the life of a semi-retired hotelier at his inn on the Costa del Sol near Málaga. Royalties from his book about CV, not to mention the holo rights and consulting fees and so on, had made him financially independent even of the inn, which was very profitable and had been for years. Local government, on the whole, was unobtrusive; the separatist problems in the north were agreeably remote.

Decent food and few worries had combined to increase Bliss's contentment as well as his girth, and so had the permanent absence of his wife, whom he had divorced in 2000, and his ne'er-do-well son, who had finally gotten some sort of job in The Gambia in 2001 and not been heard of since.

Into this little paradise a serpent came in the spring of 2005, in the form of a letter handed to him by Señorita Cortázar with his morning tea. It was from somebody named Roland Casewit III, Undersecretary of Peace in the U.S. government; it began with some complimentary phrases, then went on: "The Government of the United States would greatly value your cooperation in establishing an Expert System aboard Sea Venture in order to give the present staff the benefit of your knowledge and expertise. If it is convenient to you, we would like you to visit Sea Venture for this purpose, as the guest of the United States Government, during the last two weeks of June. Please signify your acceptance to this office as soon as possible."

"Oh, damn," said Bliss.

He couldn't turn them down, and it wouldn't be any good putting them off. "Actually, you'd like to see the old girl again, wouldn't you?" asked his friend Captain Hartman, when Bliss rang him up to complain.

"Out of curiosity, perhaps. I understand they've turned CV into a sort of prison hulk. I'd just as soon not see that, but I can't get out of it. What are you doing in June?"

"Nothing in particular. Why, would you like me to come along?"

Bliss and Hartman arrived blear-eyed in Seattle on June 15; it was eight o'clock in the evening when it ought to have been four in the morning. They were met by a cheerful young man named Corcoran, Dr. Owen's assistant, who took them in a chauffeured limousine to their hotel and showed them a few of the sights along the way. Hartman had been rather hoping to see the view from the Space Needle, but Corcoran informed him that it had been heavily damaged in a terrorist attack two years ago and had not yet been rebuilt. Feeling disoriented, the two visitors had a drink in the bar and went to bed.

In the morning after breakfast they were picked up again by Corcoran for the drive out to Sea Venture. CV, large and white as ever but looking a bit the worse for wear, was moored at the U.S. Coast Guard base in Salmon Bay. Some refitting was being done, Corcoran told them, and there were also a few bureaucratic hurdles to be dealt with before CV would cruise again.

"Is it true that you've got a prison population here?" Hartman asked.

"Oh, I wouldn't put it that way, sir. CV is a research installation now. There *is* a resident population of compulsory volunteers—we're studying them for the effects of McNulty's Disease."

They showed their boarding passes and rode up to the forward lobby, where they received temporary ID cards to be pinned on the left lapel. Then they took the elevator up to the Signal Deck, where Dr. Harriet Owen was waiting for them. She was a bit grayer than Bliss remembered her, but also more confident somehow, more in command.

"Chief Bliss and Captain Hartman, welcome," she said. "Did you have a good trip?"

"Very nice," said Bliss politely, and Hartman nodded. In fact, they were both suffering from jet lag, or jet advance you might call it, and Hartman had been barely civil at breakfast.

Owen said, "As you know, we wanted you to come here to explore the idea of putting your knowledge and experience into what the computer people call an expert system, so that in effect the computer can do just what you would have done in any foreseeable situation."

"What if the situation isn't foreseeable?" Bliss wanted to know.

"Well, that's the problem, of course, but Mr. Ewald is hoping that between you you can think of just about everything that could conceivably happen. Anyhow, it's quite an exciting idea, and I hope you'll enjoy the experience."

"Yes. By the way, I mentioned to Mr. Corcoran that I'd like to have the chance to talk to Randall Geller and Yvonne Barlow whilst I'm here."

"I know you did, and that interview will be set up for you after the session this morning."

"They're all right, I hope?"

"Oh, yes, they're fine. They send their regards."

Ewald was waiting for them in the Control Center, a chubby bald young man with an unsuccessful mustache. He had rigged up a simulator in the form of a black box with cables snaking all over: he explained that by giving simple instructions to the simulator he could display canned views on the TV screens and even, to all appearance, in the quartz deadlights, and could make any desired readings appear on the instruments. Bliss then had to look at the instruments and say what orders he would give: then Ewald would ask him why he gave them, or why he hadn't given other ones. After the first five minutes Hartman excused himself and wandered out into the Boat Deck corridors. An alert security officer said, "Excuse me, sir, are you supposed to be here?"

"I'm a visitor," Hartman said, showing his badge. "I thought I might just look round a bit."

The guard ran his minicom over the badge, looked at the readout. "This says you're supposed to be in the Control Center."

"Quite right, but it's very boring there."

The officer spoke into his phone. After a moment he got a reply, and said, "You can walk around the unrestricted areas, sir, until Mr. Bliss is ready to leave. I'm getting a security person to guide you."

"That's not necessary," Hartman said; but they waited until another guard came up, a young woman who introduced herself as Miss McMasters.

"Which are the unrestricted areas, then?" Hartman asked as they set off down the corridor. There was something institutional about the place now; the walls, which had been papered before, were now painted in blue and cream. Odd how depressing those two colors could be.

"All the public areas on the Boat Deck and Promenade Deck are unrestricted," said Miss McMasters with a cheerful smile. "Will that do?"

"Oh, certainly. Perhaps I should have asked, which areas are restricted?"

"I'm sorry, that's restricted information."

Practically no one was in the forward Boat Deck lobby except maintenance people in blue coveralls. The scientists, Hartman presumed, were in their laboratories and the prisoners in their cells. After a few more attempts to draw Miss McMasters out, Hartman gave it up and announced that he would like to leave. Miss McMasters escorted him to the exit, where his badge was taken away. Outside the checkpoint he hailed an amphicab, and spent the rest of the morning in the Olde Curiosity Shop, the Aquarium, and the charming half-timbered shops of the Olde Fishinge Village overlooking the new dike or levee or whatever they called it. A pleasing camouflage of sea air drifted from atomizers at every corner, and the smell of dead fish was hardly noticeable.

Bliss found Geller and Barlow in a small conference room near Owen's office on the Signal Deck; they looked a little thinner than he remembered them, not quite so much the carefree youth.

"Randall and Yvonne, it's good to see you," he said. They shook hands and sat down. "Is it all right to talk here?"

"You mean is it bugged?" Geller said. "I don't know. I don't care if it is or not."

"Well, are they treating you all right? Is there anything I can do?"

"They're treating us okay. Some of the others, not so good. They're breeding them like lab animals, did you know that? Trying to produce a new stock of children infected at birth."

"Surely they can't do that."

"Oh, yes, they can. We blew the whistle on them, but all that did was make them come out in the open with it. People who volunteer for the program get privileges, and people who refuse have a hard time, so they get the volunteers. But they're easy on us, for some reason. They're going to give us our old jobs in the marine lab, if we want them. Or we can just lay back and be passengers."

"They offered to let one of us go," Yvonne said.

"Namely me, because our kid drives me crazier than Yvonne. But we're selling the place in Michigan anyway, and there wouldn't be any point to it. There's a chance we can talk Owen into letting us do some of our own research. Things could be worse. What are you doing here?"

Bliss explained about the expert system. "Frankly, I wouldn't care to trust myself to it. How long do you think they'll keep you here?"

They both looked grim. "Till Geoffrey is in college, probably," said Yvonne.

"But that's monstrous! Isn't there anything you can do?"

"We have a lawyer, and he's petitioning for habeas corpus, but he says we shouldn't hold our breath."

"Well, let's look on the bright side," said Geller. "Twenty years from now, we can collaborate on a book called *Captives on CV.*"

"Not very snappy. How about *Love Slaves Afloat?*"

They smiled at each other. And, all things considered, Bliss realized, they really were all right.

A young woman came up to him at the bus stop. "Chief Bliss, I'm Ann Bonano of the Toronto *Star*. Welcome to Seattle."

"Thank you. How did you know I was here?"

"Oh, we have our methods. Staying long?"

"Just a week or so."

"And the purpose of your visit?"

Bliss explained again about the expert system. Bonano took a few notes. "That's interesting. Did you know that all the airlines are using expert systems in place of pilots now—and air controllers too?"

"No, I didn't know that," said Bliss with a shudder.

"Then is it true that you're not going to sign on again as CV's Chief of Operations?"

"Heavens, no. I'm quite content to be retired, thank you. CV was a silly thing to begin with."

"How do you mean, silly?"

"Well, you know, a prototype open sea habitat was what they called it, but it wasn't the prototype of anything. We don't need to build floating cities, the ones on land are much cheaper and more useful. The only thing sillier is L-Five, and I suppose that's why it's going forward."

Bonano thought a moment. "Do you think the pyramids were silly?"

"Yes, absolutely. Magnificently silly. You know, we seem to have this incredible urge to build large useless things. The larger the better, of course, but it really helps to put the project over if they're useless as well. I don't know why that is, do you?"

"No, I don't. Well, thank you, Mr. Bliss."

That evening he and Hartman turned on the holo and found themselves watching the Senate hearings on allegations of cruelty to CV detainees. A pale, dark-haired young man was at the witness table.

". . . have that apparatus here, and I'd like you to watch, if you would, while I demonstrate it on myself."

"We will take that under advisement," said Senator Gottlieb, a courtly white-haired man. "Now, Mr. Plotkin, you don't deny, as I understand it, that this procedure was intended to inflict intolerable pain on the subject? In order to cause the parasite to leave his body?"

"Senator, that's correct, but as you know, intolerable is a word that means different things to different people. The pain caused by this apparatus is *moderate,* I would say, but it's unpleasant. I don't know if you've ever had a bad toothache, Senator, or if anybody on the panel has? Well, that pain I would say is about twice the highest point reached on the Wolff-Wolf apparatus, and yet people endure it; I have myself. And then there's childbirth, which I *haven't* experienced." Plotkin smirked.

"The question is whether people can tolerate a pain that is natural in origin," said Senator Gottlieb, "or whether they ought to be made to tolerate a pain inflicted by somebody else. We call that torture, as you know, Mr. Plotkin."

"Except when it's done in the course of scientific research," Plotkin said.

"Then you don't call it torture?"

"No."

"Bloody barbarian," Bliss said, "they ought to shoot him."

"But surely this isn't still going on?"

"If I thought so, I wouldn't be here."

"It's a prison ship, though."

Bliss squirmed in his chair. "I know it is. I ask myself, if I refused to cooperate, what would the result be? Would they stick to this insane scheme of teaching a computer to run CV, or would they hire somebody competent?"

"There isn't anybody as competent as you."

"That's as may be. At least, if I do my job and the computer does what they say it can, it's possible that Sea Venture won't sink, prisoners and all."

Later the subcommittee allowed Plotkin to demonstrate the Wolff-Wolf machine. He put his bare arm under the lens and turned up the rheostat. "This is one dol," he said. "Just a faint prickling warmth. "This is three—this is five—seven—" The skin of his pale arm was turning pink. "This is eight." He turned the machine off.

"And is eight dols as high as you went, with the patient?"

"Yes, sir."

"Mr. Plotkin, in preparing for this demonstration, did you use any pain-killer of any kind?"

"No, sir. I did not. Anything of that kind would have been falsifying the demonstration. As a scientist, I would never do that, Senator. That would be unprincipled behavior."

Harriet Owen got up at six the next morning, an hour before her usual time, and ate her breakfast while she watched the Senate hearings in Washington. Plotkin's performance the day before had been distasteful but adequate, and he had been excused. Now, apparently, the subcommittee was considering the whole question of parasite containment. A familiar face caught her eye. "Senator," Dr. Wallace McNulty was saying, "I'd like to comment on some testimony you heard before from Mr. Peebles at NIH. If I understand what they're saying, they believe the only way to get rid of this thing is to isolate breeding populations of human beings, make sure they're free of symbionts, and forbid other people to reproduce, period. And then what?"

"As I understand Mr. Peebles' testimony," said the Chairman, "then we would expand slowly out of the quarantined areas into areas of depopulation."

"What about livestock?" McNulty asked. "Do you know the thing can go into a goat, or a fish?"

"I understand that's your belief, Doctor. If that's true, then I suppose it would be necessary to sterilize the infected areas, one at a time, before we expand into them again. I want to say that of course we all hope such extreme measures will not be needed."

"You know, this is loony," McNulty said. "You're talking about human beings as if they were laboratory animals."

The chairman was rapping his gavel. "You are out of order, Dr. McNulty."

McNulty raised his voice. "You can't get away with that, and if you could, what for?"

The chairman said, "Dr. McNulty, your remarks are out of order, and no more such outbursts will be permitted. Nevertheless, before we excuse you, I believe Senator Jergen would like to respond."

Jergen said stiffly, "What's your alternative, Doctor, just to give up and live with this parasite forever? Remember that we don't know what the long-term effects may be. There is evidence that the parasites are actually killing people in high office already. We don't know what else they are capable of. A hundred years from now we may be watching the human race go right down the slide."

McNulty said, "Senator, I take it you haven't had the disease yourself?"

"No, I haven't."

"I thought not."

"How did we ever come to this?" said Bliss. "It's fascism all over again." They were walking down the street, looking for a Greek restaurant Hartman thought he remembered seeing. Outside the carefully preserved tourist areas, the city had altered dismally since the last time Bliss had been here: plastic panels warping off the sides of buildings, some of them replaced by decaying sheets of particleboard; scabby fluepipes, scumbled blue and red, hanging all anyhow from building faces; filth, grime, rubbish heaped in corners.

*"Plus ça change,* the more it's the same old mess," Hartman said. "If you look back far enough, what we now call national governments all began as protection rackets, pure and simple."

A ragged man lurched toward them out of a doorway. "Spare a fiver, boss? I haven't ate since yesterday." Hartman fumbled out a plastic coin and gave it to him.

"Thanks, boss," said the man. There was something wrong with his face; it was grey and sweaty. He went away with a stumbling gait.

"Probably spend it on drugs," Bliss said.

"No doubt. Well, as I was saying, you've heard about protection? A gangster stops by and tells you that for five hundred dollars a month he'll protect you against vandalism. If you turn him down, you know somebody will break your windows. So you pay. The same thing happened thousands of years ago, when people stopped hunting and gathering and took up agriculture. As soon as there were large fixed populations of farmers, they became a profit source for bandits. The bandits farmed the farmers. They said, turn over a share of what you produce, and we'll protect you against other bandits. And they did, you know, but if they hadn't, the next lot would have been no worse. Then the bandits fought each other for territory, and presently there were warlords and dukes and so on. The imperial palaces in China were built on the rice extorted from peasants. So the peasants, who had had plenty for themselves, were reduced to poverty, and the imperial court got rich. When England and France went to war in the fourteenth century, they were disputing the right to farm the French peasants. We've always had the two classes, the one that produces and the one that takes."

"Aren't you a member of the class that takes?"

"I am not, I'm a working man like yourself. Now mind you, the system produced some marvelous things. The glory that was Greece and so on. But it certainly has altered our moral perceptions. I remember when the controversy over the Aswan Dam was going on, somebody said that the irrigation projects were good on balance because they produced more food. And somebody else replied that it was the people in the cities who got the food, and the peasants who got bilharziasis."

"But don't you think it's better for some people to be rich, or at least comfortably off, than for everybody to be poor?"

"That's my point, the peasants *weren't* poor until the gangsters took them over. Nowadays there are no more peasants in this part of the world, and nobody asked for

their opinion anyhow, but how many would have agreed
to that proposition, do you suppose?"

"I take your point, but that's all water under the
bridge."

"Ah, but it isn't. The question is being reopened, you
see, because the parasites are beginning to kill people
who kill other people. Presently the gangsters won't be
able to use force any longer. If everybody agrees that it's
better for some to be rich and the rest to be poor, then
nothing will change. But I don't think so, do you?"

After a week and a half Bliss and Hartman got on a
plane and went home, Bliss to Spain and Hartman to
England.

Later that year the Senate subcommittee returned a
report declaring that the detention of McNulty's victims, and the pain experiments thereon, were justified
under the powers of the Emergency Civil Control Authority, but requesting the President to instruct the
experimenters to use more humane methods in future,
whenever possible. Sea Venture, with its complement of
scientists, security people and detainees, went to sea in
November.

**2** In her kindergarten classroom on the Main Deck, Andrea Ottenburg said, "Story time! Let's make a big circle." She waited for the scraping of red and blue chairs to stop. When the children were quiet and attentive, she began, "Once there was a marvelous big boat that thousands of people could live on and float around and around the Pacific Ocean. The boat could float on top of the water or underneath it. And do you know what the boat was called?"

"CV!" a dozen voices chorused.

"Yes! And we're all on that marvelous boat right now. But something funny happened on CV a few years ago. This was before any of you were here. An invisible fairy got on board the boat, and it could get into people's minds and make them think differently. And people were frightened at first because when the fairy left them to go to somebody else, the people fell into a deep sleep."

"Like Snow White," said Linda.

"Exactly! But they woke up again after about a week, and so people weren't so frightened anymore. But they still didn't know if it was a good fairy or a bad fairy, so they fooled it with a goat dressed up in a person's clothes. And the fairy went into the goat, and then do you know what?"

Peter's hand was raised. "They put it in a box."

"Yes, and what did they do with the box?"

Three hands were up. "Yes, Sylvia?"

"They sunk it in the ocean."

"Yes, they *sank* it in the ocean. But that wasn't the last of the fairies, was it?"

Heads were shaking.

"No, because when the next baby was born, another fairy was born with it. And then other babies were born and other fairies."

Linda's hand was up. "Does everybody have a fairy?"

"No, there aren't that many fairies."

Another hand. "Mrs. Ottenburg, are they good fairies or bad fairies?"

"Well, we don't know that yet for *sure.* That's why we're all here on CV, because we want to find out."

There was a little silence. Then Peter, the bravest, said, "If they're good fairies, why do they want to kill them?"

"They don't want to kill them, just put them to sleep." Oh. She saw the look of comprehension in their faces. They were buying it, for now: but all this hypocrisy would have to be undone later—at what cost?

Andrea Ottenburg, who liked to speak her mind even though she was a detainee, expressed her concerns to Melanie Kurtz, the chief of kindergarten and preschool education. Kurtz agreed with her and brought the matter up at a conference later that week.

"What Andrea and some of the other teachers are concerned about," said Kurtz, "is that this program runs counter to our commitment to teach children as early as possible to distinguish fantasy from reality. There are some things we have to shield them from, of course, but it really is disturbing that we're introducing imaginary entities, which we're going to have to tell them later don't exist. Pedagogically this is a very counterproductive thing, and I just wonder if we've looked hard enough for another solution."

"It really isn't possible to discuss the parasite realistically, at that age, though, is it?" Harriet Owen asked. "What do you think, Dwayne?"

"No, of course we can't do that, and it is necessary to tell them something that will tend to quiet their anxieties," Dwayne Swarts said. "Fortunately or unfortunately, they all know what fairies are, and so that seems like the obvious way to go about it."

"I don't agree," Dorothy Italiano said. *"I* don't think fantasy is bad for children."

Kurtz turned to her. "Do you want to teach them to believe in Santa Claus?"

"Not especially, but I think I really understand why parents want to deceive their children in that way, and other ways. They sense that fantasy is *important;* they want the children to have the feeling that there are wonderful things in the world. Maybe they have to stop believing in fairies later, although there are places in the world where grown people still do, but at least they'll have had that sense of wonder, of magic."

"I can't agree with that. I think children should be taught the truth."

"Even if it makes them cry themselves to sleep?"

Kurtz said nothing. The conference came to no conclusion, and the kindergarten teachers went on telling their children about fairies.

In the R&D section on "K" Deck, Rick Adams, a new assistant, was getting an orientation lecture from his boss. Adams was skimpy and dark, Glen Cunningham tall and blond. Both of them wore white lab coats, but Adams had more pens in his pocket.

"Let's look at what we know about the parasite," Glen Cunningham said. "One, it can't pass through a solid object. We know that by experiment and inference—the original parasite came out of a capsule that was found at the bottom of the ocean, and apparently had been there for a long time, but it came out only when the capsule was broken.

"So that brings us to the second point. The parasite can't leave an unconscious person. The fact that totally blind people seem to be immune to McNulty's suggests a reason why—the parasite has to have some sensory input from its host about the location of another possible host. When the host's eyes are closed, well, it can't get that information. We have one trial in which it appears that the parasite *can* use other sensory information such as touch—the parasite apparently didn't pass through the space between the two hosts, but they were touching at the time, and we think it may have moved along the nerves of one host until it reached the other. Normally, though, we think the parasite is resident in the brain. In every other trial it has come out of the host's skull and entered the same way."

"What about the solid object rule there?" Adams asked.

"The skull isn't a totally closed object. There's a direct route to the brain through the nasal passages, for instance. Anyway, number three, we know the parasite reproduces in human females, apparently at the time of conception, and we know by experiment that it can also reproduce in laboratory animals. Experiments with fish are inconclusive so far, but there is some reason to believe that the parasite needs a host with a fairly complex nervous system—it couldn't invade a plant, for instance, and probably not an insect or arachnid.

"Fourth, we know the parasite can't travel more than about four feet between hosts. That might be a limitation of time instead of distance, we don't know yet, but the fact is well established.

"So these are the limitations we know the parasite has, and it's our job to exploit them in any way we can. And if we can find any others, we'll hit them too. Sound interesting?"

"Sure does. One question?"

"Okay."

"It sounds like the parasite is ahead so far. What happens if we don't catch up?"

"Oh, little things like the end of Western civilization."

**3** In a house on a quiet street in Brussels, a little girl named Marie-Claude was standing on a chair to reach a sugarbowl on the counter. The observer was fascinated by the brightness of the image of sugar in her mind, the memory of piercing sweetness, as compelling as sex was for an adult. She took the lid off and put her fingers in, but the bowl tipped and spilled sugar, sparkling white grains heaped on the counter. A sound made her turn. There was Maman, a red-faced giant. "I told you not to do that!"

Fear was like an electric current that crisped her body. "I didn't mean to!"

The woman's hand closed around her wrist, yanked her off the chair. "Now you're going to be punished!"

Hot tears blurred her vision; the catastrophe was unattended, unthought of, a reality that blotted out all else. She was being dragged across the floor, held upright by the painful grip on her arm, across the kitchen into the bathroom. Then she was bent across the woman's lap, and she slipped out across the grey space and in again, and felt the ungoverned fury as she brought the hairbrush down on the child's buttocks, *paf!* and again, and again.

In a cold schoolroom in Leeds, Miss McDevitt said, "Quentin, you're to stay after."

The rest of them trooped out, some with knowing backward glances, and he was alone with Miss McDevitt. She picked up a paper from her desk. "This was the question," she said. " 'How do you know you have a country?' And you wrote, 'Same way I know the world is round.' "

Quentin Morris said nothing. He was eleven, skinny in a ragged sweater.

"How *dare* you!" Miss McDevitt picked up another paper and another. "Sally answered the question without being insolent, and so did Brian, and so did Malcolm and Nigel and all the others." Her mouth was flecked with spittle. "What makes you so very exceptional? I'd like to hear."

Quentin mumbled something.

"What? Speak up."

"I just meant it was hearsay."

"What do you mean, hearsay?"

"I have a country, and the world is round. I know it because other people tell me."

Miss McDevitt put the papers down and looked at him. "You know very well that isn't what we're talking about. We're talking about patriotism, and pride, and love of king and country. But I suppose you wouldn't know about any of those things, would you, Quentin? All right, you can go."

As he turned, the observer felt the tears stinging his eyelids, and he slipped out across the grey space and in again, feeling the familiar shock. She watched the boy close the door behind him. He was intelligent, talented no doubt, in a degenerate way—and he was mocking her. The idea infuriated her again, and she thought of all the things she would like to do to the little beast, if the school code did not forbid. Make him sit in a corner with a dunce cap on his head. Cane him.

The room was very still. She thought of her lonely supper, and the papers to be corrected. Moving slowly, she gathered her things, put on her weather shoes, hat and coat, picked up her umbrella, turned out the lights and locked the door behind her. The corridor shone slick and empty, still echoing with the clatter of voices.

Out in the street, the rain was persistent, drenching and cold; it was June, but spring had not yet come. She put up her umbrella and walked past the noisy pupils waiting to board the school buses. She glimpsed Quentin at the end of the queue; he did not look up.

She kept on, past the tobacconist's and the cube shop, down to the municipal bus shelter beyond the next crossing. In her mind there was a fantasy picture, quite bright and detailed: she had bent the boy over a chair and tied his hands. Now she pulled his trousers down, exposing the piteous pale buttocks. She let him wait awhile. Then she drew the cane back for the first stroke: *whack!* The bus drew up, spraying sick yellow light from its windows; the doors rattled open. As she climbed aboard, she slipped out with relief and into the driver as she put her card in the slot: he was a Jamaican who hated the country and the weather, and as he closed the door and pushed the drive button he was thinking with hatred of his wife and her eternal fried bangers. At the next stop he slipped out again into a passenger, an elderly accountant named Elkins; there was something wrong with his back, an old injury, and he was belching the essence of the bad fish he had eaten at lunch.

From Leeds the observer went to London by rail in a banker named Forrester, whose recollections of duck-hunting as a boy were very interesting; then he found an attractive young woman who wanted to be pregnant, and stayed in her until that was accomplished. Her next host was an elderly painter traveling by Chunnel to Paris; although she was physically frail, her perceptions of color and light were much more vivid than any the observer had yet known, and she cherished them to give to others.

Every human being was a unique blend of thought and emotion. In almost every one, no matter how life had deformed or corrupted them, there was an understratum of love and longing for their wounded planet. They knew so much! but their knowledge was divided: one knew banking, another art, another agriculture. Even when they understood what was wrong, they seemed helpless.

Far more often now than in the past, she found herself in a mind already inhabited by others of her race. It happened in Paris, in the mind of a boulevardier who was thinking rather dull thoughts about his mistresses.

If only they could share as we do!    Some do, a little.
                                   But they don't know it.
                              Open them up?
      Trying, with the newborns.
        It's harder than we thought.
          Our parent could have told us
            if she had lived.                    *Sorrow.*

And indeed, there was sorrow in all of them, never quite absent. Their parent, the wise one: how many mistakes were they making because they had never known her?

**4** In Huanchaca, Bolivia, Juan Montoya accepted the carton from the man ahead of him, passed it back. The warehouse doors stood open; all the food was coming out, in two streams, hand to hand to hand. Down below there were mule carts, a tractor with a flatbed trailer, two or three pickups, farm wagons, even bicycles.

Opposite Montoya were three militia, looking on with angry faces. They couldn't do anything. Montoya laughed and gestured with his chin. The tall one started as if he had been struck. He unslung his rifle, raised it to his shoulder, then fell slowly across it and lay in the dust. The other two bent toward him. They crossed themselves, picked up the dead man. One of them said over his shoulder, "God will punish you."

Montoya said cheerfully, "Then why did He never punish you?" The soldier turned his face away.

In Dr. Owen's computer tube, calls were stacked up: Maintenance, a Philippine reporter, nothing she felt like responding to right now. Another appeared: Glen Cunningham, with the flag, "D&D." That might be interesting.

"Mitzi, Glen," she said to the computer.

Cunningham's head appeared in the tube. "I think we've got something on the d-and-d project," he said.

"Really? Tell me about it."

"Well, one of the problems we had with the old system, it was based on the assumption that the parasite would move in a direct line between one host and another. Then we could set up our apparatus at the right place and destroy it. But it turns out that when you shock the host, the parasite can emerge in a random direction—it doesn't necessarily go toward the nearest host."

"So what's the answer, Glen?"

"Rick Adams came up with this—he suggested that if the parasite is some kind of stable energy system, it may have a net charge, and in that case it ought to be possible to draw it out with a strong magnetic field. We tried it, and it checks out in three trials so far. Here's the apparatus." He moved back and showed her a device on a tall framework. "This electromagnet generates a field of two hundred oersted. The neat part is that we don't have to use electroshock or anything invasive to the host. We put the subject's head against the magnet and turn it on. The parasite, if it's there, comes out and is held by the magnet; then we zap it with twenty thousand volts, and that's all she wrote."

"That's marvelous, Glen. One question, how do you verify that the parasite is destroyed?"

He looked embarrassed. "Only by trying to infect another host, so far. We'd prefer a more positive method, and there might be a way to detect the energy released by the parasite when it's destroyed, but the way we're killing it rules that out. We're still working on it. We'll come up with something."

"I'm sure you will, and meanwhile you're doing marvelously. You want me to forward this to the National Laboratories?"

"Yes, and recommend a field trial."

"I'll certainly do that. Good work, Glen."


Aaron Burstyn, an experimental detainee, was watching the holo in his cell.

"We're talking to Harold W. Geiger, the president of General Motors. Mr. Geiger, there's an interesting and controversial thing you've introduced in your plants recently. You're trying to motivate your workers to greater productivity by giving them free brain implants which can then be used to stimulate their pleasure centers, or other centers, by the use of a device that provides a metered dosage in their off-work hours. Do I have that right?"

"Yes, that's about it, Bob. As you know, we've been very, very concerned about turnover and worker morale for several years. This looked like something that might improve those problems."

"And how is it working out?"

"Well, we're very encouraged, but it's too soon to say."

"About how many workers—what percentage—have signed up for the brain implants?"

"It's small so far; that's why I can't be definite about results as of yet."

"By small do you mean ten percent? Five? One?"

"It's in that range."

"So you would say there is some resistance to the idea of brain implants?"

"There's always resistance to anything new, Bob, as you know."

"All right. Now, what's to prevent someone who has had this implant from stimulating his own brain whenever he feels like it?"

"Well, the implant has a gadget in it, so it only lets the current through into your brain when it gets a certain kind of signal. In other words, you put this cap on your head, and it's like a bank account—there are so many seconds of stimulation that you've earned by productivity and low absenteeism and so on. There's a formula, which we're still working out with the union. So it's really like a bonus for good performance, and the beauty part of it is, is that it doesn't harm the worker or lead to the problems we're trying to correct, like alcohol or drugs do."

"What about bootleg decoding devices? There have been some rumors about that."

"We're trying to run down those rumors, but at this point in time I'd say that's just what they are."

"Mr. Geiger, what kind of pleasure does a person experience under this stimulation? Have you tried it yourself?"

"No, I personally haven't tried it, but I understand it's usually just a general kind of pleasure—the way you feel when you're relaxed and have no worries."

"We've heard that the implant can stimulate other areas—make a person feel the way they do under the influence of alcohol, for example."

"There is a certain amount of choice involved. We try

to give people what they want. And, of course, if a person does choose the option you just mentioned, they get all the fun of having a mild buzz on without any of the bad effects."

"Can they have a cocaine high, too, without the cocaine?"

"It's possible."

"A sexual experience?"

"That's possible too."

"Some of these experiences can be highly addictive, can't they?"

"There is no addiction whatsoever, because we're not giving them drugs in any shape or form."

"But speaking generally, wouldn't you say that a person who has grown used to these experiences would feel deprived if they had to give them up?"

"Well, there are a lot of things like that. Money, for instance."

"Mr. Geiger, say I'm a worker in one of your plants and I decide to quit for some reason. What happens to my brain implant?"

"Well, you can have it removed if you want, or you can just leave it in. It can't do any harm."

"But I can't use it anymore?"

"No, not unless you've earned it."

"Thank you, Mr. Geiger."

"My pleasure."


Melanie Kurtz made a point of spending some time every day in one of the ten kindergarten classes, sometimes working with the children, sometimes watching behind the one-way glass. She had deliberately not familiarized herself with the names and faces of children in the breeding program, who presumably had acquired the parasite at birth, but she could not help trying to guess which ones they were. The whole point, after all, was to try to find out what difference there was between the two populations. She believed in objectivity and rigor, but she also believed in insight.

"There's one," said Lou Willows, who was on duty today behind the mirror in Kindergarten 8. "Hedy, the girl in the red jumper, over there with the ball?"

"Why do you say that?" Kurtz asked, although she thought she knew.

"Look at her. See how she's watching Denny? He's the one who was crying a minute ago." Denny had been playing with the big blue and white ball when another boy took it away from him. Then the second kid threw the ball away, and a minute later Hedy had it. The teacher, a conscientious young woman named Levin, had soothed Denny and given him a truck to play with, and the whole thing had been smoothed over. But Hedy kept glancing over at Denny. Now she stood up, fanny higher than her head for a moment. She walked straight over to Denny and put the ball down in the bed of his truck. Denny knocked it away with his fist, then got up and pursued it. Hedy watched him a moment, then picked up the truck and walked away.

"Now how do you figure that?" asked Lou.

"Pretty smart."

"At two, she'd have to be a genius. I think there's something else. Sure, she wanted the truck, and she got it. But she gave the ball to Denny because she knew he wanted it."

"ESP?"

"Why does it have to be ESP? She could tell by his behavior."

"Yes, and you could be projecting, too."

"I know that, and I know we're not supposed to guess, but I'd be inhuman if I didn't wonder."

**5** In a conference room at SARP, a military think-tank in Akademgorodok, seven high-ranking officers were gathered. Their host was Colonel Professor Arpad Adjarian. The others were representatives of the Russian Army, Navy and Air Force. "During the past year," Adjarian told them, "there have been over four hundred known cases of the sudden death of a commander at the moment when he was about to give an order for troops to fire or weapons to be launched. In all cases there was no visible sign of violence. The official cause of death, when one was given, was heart failure.

"Our staff has carefully compared these reports, and we find that in more than two hundred cases the subordinate who stepped forward to fill his superior's position also fell dead. We have sixty cases in which the same thing happened to a third officer. After that, in all cases, action was abandoned.

"These cases can no longer be dismissed as coincidence. As the Americans say, 'Once is an accident, twice is coincidence, three times is evidence of hostile activity.' We must conclude that there is a force in the world that does not wish war to be fought by conventional methods, a force that is able and willing to impose its will. I point out that these deaths have occurred all over the world, in the socialist as well as the imperialist camps. We are dealing, in other words, with a third force, as yet unknown."

"But what is this force?" asked General Vasyutin. "You can't simply call it 'unknown.'"

"As to that, there are three hypotheses. I will argue in a moment, Comrade General, that our response must be the same no matter what the nature of our enemy, but to reply to your question: First, an international organization, using new weapons, which has infiltrated the armed forces of every nation and even government officials at high levels. Second, after all, that it is merely a series of coincidental events. Third, that these deaths are caused by the so-called McNulty's Virus acting in a coordinated way to achieve its ends."

"I don't believe in invisible intelligences."

"Nor do I, Comrade General, but as Marxists and scientists we must adhere to the principle of least hypothesis. All three of these possibilities are incredible, but the third is a little less incredible than the others."

"Let us see if we can test this hypothesis," said General Durnovo. "If the virus is responsible, why did it begin to act five years after it first appeared?"

"That is accounted for in principle by the progress of the epidemic. According to World Health Organization estimates, there are now approximately two hundred million individual viruses in the world. It may be that this represents a critical value. There are enough viruses, distributed through the world population, to enforce their will wherever they wish. This accords with the fact that in the last six months no command to inflict lethal damage on enemy forces has gone unpunished. Earlier episodes may be accounted for by unusually large local concentrations of virus."

"Counterrevolutionaries," muttered General Usakov, a grizzled veteran of the Afghan War.

"With all respect, Comrade General, counterrevolutionaries that act impartially against socialists and imperialists alike? But I say again that in the last analysis it does not matter who or what this force is. We have only two options, to neutralize the third force or to adapt ourselves to it successfully."

"Assuming that you are right," said Vasyutin, "which option do you recommend?"

"Both. The Americans and British have developed methods of detecting and destroying the viruses. We have obtained samples of these devices, and Russian scientists are working to improve them. There is a chance that because of our superior organization we will be able to use such devices more effectively than the capitalists, but at the same time we are hampered in a fundamental sense by the vast extent of our territory. Therefore in the short term I believe we must revise our methods in such a way that we can achieve our objectives without violence. Fortunately, there are clear indications that this can be done."

Adjarian pressed a button. "Here is a possible model of the new Russian infantryman." In the holotube a man appeared, wearing a lightweight uniform and a helmet with a transparent visor. In his right hand he carried a long pole with a metal apparatus at the end; in his left, a net.

"A *retiarius,*" said Kondakov. "There is his net, and that other thing looks like a trident. Are you really proposing that we go back to Roman times?"

"Quite right. The weapon which you compare to a trident is the device developed by the Americans to subdue and isolate carriers of the virus." He pressed the button again. On the screen another man appeared, dressed as a civilian. The soldier stepped forward, leveled his weapon and thrust it at the other man's waist. The device at the end of the pole locked around the captive. The soldier dragged him away.

"That's all very well for an unarmed man," said Vasyutin, "but what does it have to do with combat?"

"If the other man were conventionally armed," replied Adjarian, "his weapons would be useless. Under the assumptions we are discussing, if he even formed the intention of killing our infantryman, let's say with a rifle or a grenade, he would fall dead."

"And if he had the same weapons as our man?"

"For that, we have a computer simulation that is quite interesting."

In the holotube, a rolling landscape appeared. Two armed bodies of men were approaching each other through the scattered trees, some in personnel carriers, others on foot. One group was in blue uniforms, the other in brown. The footsoldiers were variously armed, some with shields and long poles with padded tips, others with "tridents" and nets.

As the two groups closed, mortars on either side began firing. The projectiles were large white objects; when they struck the enemy, the latter were knocked down, and the projectiles burst, releasing clouds of white powder.

"Pillow fights?" said General Usakov incredulously. "I've seen enough."

"I hope you'll stay until the demonstration is over. I understand your feeling, Comrade General, but kindly reserve judgment. By the way," Adjarian added, "those white clouds you see do not represent chemical agents, but simply chalk dust, intended to confuse the enemy and reduce his range of vision."

Now water cannons were bowling over men on either side. A hail of rubber bullets spun them around. Then the two sides had closed. The shieldmen thrust at the opponents with their padded poles; the retiarii thrust with their tridents. Whenever a man fell, a retiarius was there to tangle him in a net or capture him with a trident.

The watching officers observed that when two shieldmen were engaged, a retiarius could circle around one of them and bring him down; conversely, when two retiarii faced each other, a shieldman with his longer weapon could knock one of the combatants off his feet.

When the brief engagement was over, the brown army was mopping up. The remaining blue soldiers were surrounded, netted or secured with tridents, and led away to the rear.

"I see that we shall have to read our Vegetius again," said Vasyutin.

"Indeed," responded Adjarian, "and very carefully. Well, comrades, of course this is only a simulation, but from it we learn that in an encounter between two forces armed with the same weapons, discipline, strength, and numbers will prevail. That is somewhat reassuring. Weapons change, but war is still war."

"What if your enemy is not on foot, but in tanks and armored carriers?"

"I might reply that in that case, we would be in tanks and carriers too, but a better question is, what can men in tanks and carriers accomplish? Tanks can push down obstacles and destroy buildings, true, but in doing so they will kill people, and the soldiers in them will die. In any event, at some point in any engagement, the soldiers must get out of their vehicles in order to achieve their objective of subduing the enemy, and then the situation is as before."

"What about aircraft?" demanded an officer with silver wings on his lapels.

"To drop chemical agents and smokescreens, certainly. We'll have to investigate that sort of thing carefully. There may be an advantage in using these methods when a commander is faced by troops better trained or more numerous than his own. But it's also possible that they would only confuse and delay the issue. Here we can draw on the lessons of the First Imperialist War. At any rate, we'll certainly need light, low-flying aircraft for reconnaissance and diversion, but—under these assumptions—heavy bombers and fighters are a thing of the past."

"And the Navy?" asked Admiral Levachevsky.

"For transport, support operations and intelligence gathering, yes. But to the extent that the Navy exists to inflict mortal damage on the enemy, it too is a thing of the past."

Afterward Vasyutin, who happened to be Adjarian's father-in-law, came to the Colonel's office, closed the door and sat down rather heavily. "Arpad," he said, "I am very tired. Be so kind as to give me a cigarette."

Adjarian pushed the cigarette box across his desk and offered a lighter.

Puffing smoke, Vasyutin resumed, "You know, I couldn't help thinking as you spoke that the problem you described so well is even more acute in internal security than in the armed forces. After all, one has to fight a war every fifteen or twenty years, but security matters go on by day and night."

"True, Trofim Semyonich," said Adjarian, "but fortunately that's not your concern or mine."

"No, it isn't. But I think you should know that unusual deaths among the KGB have been a matter for serious concern in the Kremlin for over a year. There have also been some unexplained fatalities in the Party apparatus in Volgograd, in Novosibirsk, and other places. This is not public knowledge, of course, and I count on your discretion."

"Of course, that goes without saying."

"How is Natashka, by the way? And the children?"

"Very well, thank you. Petya is a big boy now, you would not recognize him."

"I wanted to get out to see you all while I was here, but it's impossible. I am flying back to Moscow in an hour." Vasyutin drew meditatively on his cigarette. After a moment he went on, "I'm inclined to believe you when you say the virus is responsible. As you say, one hypothesis is more fantastic than the other, but this one is a little less fantastic. What worries me is the question, can the state be held together without violence?" He waved a hand. "Don't bother to tell me that it ought to be. My question is, *can* it be?"

Adjarian was silent.

Vasyutin continued for a moment in English, "You know, perhaps, what Dr. Samuel Johnson said? 'Patriotism is the last refuge of a scoundrel.' Of course *he* didn't mean that patriotism is a bad thing, but in fact it is one of the worst things in the world. Patriotism is that emotion that persuades young men to be killed in a war; it has no other use. We are taught to love our country, but as I grow older, I realize more and more that one cannot love a country, only land and people.

"Now I'm going to tell you something else, and this you must regard as absolutely confidential. Somehow the rumors of these KGB deaths have got out. There have been incidents . . . Last week in Moscow a gang of hooligans attacked a 'bread truck' in broad daylight, pulled out the driver and two guards, beat them up, and released five prisoners while a crowd watched. They are still at large, both the hooligans and the prisoners. What I want to know is, if there are no prisoners and no jailers, can there be a Russian state? Well, well, Arpad, we live in interesting times, to be sure." He stood up. "Until later, dear boy. Give my love to Natalya."

Adjarian went home to his dacha, greeted his wife and children, and sat down in the garden with a pipe to wait for supper. Comforting sounds and smells came from the kitchen. The apple tree was in bloom; the evening sky was pure. A mood of melancholy came over him: how terrible it would be to leave all this!

He was just over forty, a rising man with solid

accomplishments behind him. Arms, strategy, tactics, military history and philosophy, however, were all he knew. The words of his father-in-law came back to him: "If there are no prisoners and no jailors, can there be a Russian state?"

Or, for that matter, any state?

Adjarian considered himself a realist, and he knew that the problems they were facing went far beyond the military aspect.

If his views were correct they would eventually prevail, and his position would be more secure than ever. But if the foundations of the Republic were crumbling?

Adjarian thought of the brutally repressed "Moscow Spring" of seventeen years ago, of the Gulag and Lubyanka Prison, the censorship of newspapers, the gray hand of bureaucracy everywhere. As an Armenian, he knew exactly how much love for the Russians there was in the Autonomous Okrugs still remaining within the Russian Federated Socialist Republic. What if the state could no longer keep ethnic and nationalist enthusiasm under control? Or what if, in spite of everything, patriotism became outmoded—war itself impossible?

In the house he heard Piotr quarreling with his sister. Then his wife's calm voice, and after a moment a burst of laughter. Adjarian smiled.

**6** One morning Dwayne Swarts called Italiano and asked her to lunch. "I warn you I want to ask for a favor," he said.

They met in the staff dining room at one. "I'll get right to the point," said Swarts. "I have a patient I think you might help me with. His name is Geoffrey Barlow-Geller; he's four years old. Emotional lability, inappropriate behavior in class, doesn't interact with the other children. Intelligence tests are ambiguous because of his attention span, but my guess is he's normal or above. They did a workup on him before they sent him to me; no physical problems."

"I know the parents, and I've seen Geoffrey from a distance. What do they say?"

"He's always been like this. Weepy, very dependent, hard to deal with. I asked them if there's anything that seems to calm him down, and they told me he likes three things. He likes being held, he likes noisy toys, and he likes loud music. I've tried to persuade him to tell me what's bothering him, and all he'll say is, 'Too much talking.' I heard that the obvious way at first, but then it turns out that he says the same thing when he's been crying in his room all by himself. What does that sound like to you, just offhand?"

"Paranoid schiz? Voices in his head?"

"It might be. If I can't think of anything else, I'm going to have to start him on a course of carphenazine."

"Well, Dwayne, what can I do?"

"You've hypnotized children, haven't you?"

"Yes, occasionally."

"Okay, I know it's a long shot, but I'd like you to put him into trance and see if you can find out if he does hear voices. If that isn't it, I don't want to give him inappropriate medication. Can you do it—have you got time?"

"Yes, I'll try."

Geoffrey Barlow-Geller was an unattractive little boy —head too big for his body, nose runny, eyelids pink and swollen. He cried when his mother left him in Italiano's office, and put his hands over his ears when she tried to talk to him. Eventually she got his attention with a toy robot that whirred and blinked its eyes. She let him play with it awhile, then put it on the desk and stopped the motor.

"See the robot, Geoffrey? Look how bright its eyes are. Look at the robot's eyes, they're getting brighter and brighter, aren't they? Keep on looking at the robot's eyes, and now you can feel that you're getting sleepy. You're getting sleepier and sleepier, and now you feel like closing your eyes. Yes, and now you're getting sleepier, but you can still hear my voice . . . ."

She got him into light trance, gave him an induction cue, told him he would always feel good after these sessions, and brought him out of it.

The second session was much the same. In the third

session, she was able to talk him down into deep trance, demonstrated by arm rigor and glove anesthesia.

She said, "Geoffrey, are you hearing voices in your head now?"

A pause. "Yes."

"All right. In a moment, when I say 'Begin,' you're going to find it's very easy to tell me what the voices are saying. It doesn't matter whether you understand them or not. If they talk too fast for you, you'll just repeat as much as you can, and that's all right. Do you understand?"

"Yes."

"All right. Begin."

Geoffrey's lips parted. His voice was childish, but the words were not. ". . . this here one, onna otha hand, I could letcha have fuh fifty dollas . . . don't you just *try* not to be such a son of a . . . sehpa zeenatrositay, sehteen soteez . . . over the last six months, about an eleven percent rise, but I think you'd best . . . soong poo cow jee, wo ming tyen lie kan . . . get this terrible heartburn about half an hour after . . . tengaw see gemoo eetoo, selula deea makan nasee . . . thing I'd ever seen, and now she looks like a . . ."

When the boy began to show signs of distress, Italiano gave him permission to stop. "Now when I count to three, you're going to wake up. And you'll wake up feeling good, and you'll find out that the voices won't bother you so much. You'll still hear them, but you won't have to pay attention. They'll be just like voices in the next room, and you won't have to listen. You can do whatever you want, talk, or listen to people who are really in the room, and the voices won't bother you. One, two, three." Geoffrey's eyes opened.

"Feel all right?"

"Yes." He smiled.

Alone in her office, Italiano played the recording back with a prickling of fear up her spine. Whatever this was, it was not like any auditory hallucination she had ever heard of. There was no delusional content, no relevance at all; the words were like random bits of holo conversations. She was especially puzzled by the parts that were not English; they were too structured to be random babbling or glossolalia. It was difficult to tell because of the childish accent, but one part sounded to her for all the world like French.

Through the computer she found a French-speaking detainee and played the recording for him. When it was done, she said, "Is there anything there that you recognized?"

"Yes, of course. *'C'est pas une atrocité, c'est une sottise.'* That means, 'It isn't an atrocity, it is a stupidity.'"

"Are you sure?"

"Oh, yes. It was very clear."

"Was there anything else that you recognized, except for the English?"

"No, but I heard one part that I think is an Oriental language. Perhaps more than one."

"Thank you, Mr. Lagritte."

Through the computer again, she found a Chinese-American businessman who had spent a good deal of time in the Far East. She played the recording for him. "Did you recognize any of that, Mr. Sun?"

"Oh, yes. 'Send notice by mail, tomorrow I come see you.' "

"What language is that?"

"Chinese. Mandarin."

"Anything else?"

"Yes. Another part is either Indonesian or Malaysian. 'Look at Fatty, he's always eating.' " He giggled. "Not very nice."

In subsequent sessions, some of them attended by Dwayne Swarts, she got more of the same kind of material, and sent recordings to linguists ashore. One passage turned out to be Finnish, another Russian; there were still others that nobody could identify.

"I think it's clear," she told Dr. Owen, "that this is some kind of telepathy. I know how that sounds, but the other hypotheses are absolutely ruled out."

"We have a polyglot population here, not to mention what he could have been exposed to earlier."

"Yes, I know, and there have been cases where a trance subject has been able to reproduce written materials in other languages, sometimes with astonishing accuracy, just from having glimpsed them in a book somewhere, but this isn't *like* that. From all we can find out, Geoffrey is hearing these voices in his head pretty much all the time, and that's what's the matter with him."

"So you think these are real voices, in some sense— he's picking up people's thoughts as they speak?"

"That's what it looks like."

"Any idea who the speakers are?"

"No. There was one case where the speaker was complaining of heartburn after meals, and I checked with the MDs on board. None of them had had a patient with heartburn on that day, although it's a common complaint. We don't have anybody on board who speaks Finnish or Russian. And there was something about sending a message by mail. There hasn't been any mail service in the U.S. for ten years, and we certainly don't have it here. In itself, that's not surprising; all the studies show that telepathy doesn't depend on distance. But there has never been any report of telepathy taking this extended auditory form. People hear their name called, or they get hunches, or see visions, but this is like being plugged into a phone system with crossed wires. No wonder the poor kid is desperate."

"You said you'd given him suggestions that he won't mind the voices so much. How has that worked out?"

"Not very well. He's doing a little better in school and at home, but he still cries a lot."

"All right, Dorothy, this is interesting, but why is it important?"

Italiano hesitated. "Geoffrey was born right around the time the new outbreak of McNulty's started. He may be a primary host, and if he is, this may be the kind of thing we're going to see more of."

"That's two maybes, but I see your point. You're right, of course. We ought to study him carefully, if only to anticipate things that may happen in the primary host population later on. Do you have any suggestions?"

"I'd like to test him for other paranormal abilities. We don't know yet that this is the only thing he can do. And of course we ought to run all the other tests we can think of—EEG, basal, and so on. Poor thing, he's going to be a busy little boy."

"Maybe it will take his mind off the voices."

After three attempts, Geller succeeded in getting Owen on the phone.

"Hello, Mr. Geller," she said. "I understand there's some problem about Geoffrey."

"Some problem! They told us to get him ready for brain surgery!"

"Please be calm, Mr. Geller. What we're proposing is a very simple, safe procedure. It's been performed on thousands of people for therapy and even for recreational use."

"I don't care how many—"

"All we're going to do is to insert an electrode into Geoffrey's auditory center so that we can blank out those voices he's hearing—or rather, so that he can do it himself, just by pressing a button. We're trying to help him, Mr. Geller and Ms. Barlow."

"We believe that's for us to decide," Barlow said. Her lips were thin. "We'd like to make a formal request for all three of us to be discharged so that we can take Geoffrey to our own doctors."

"That will be denied. Honestly, Ms. Barlow, he is getting far better medical attention here than you could ever afford to pay for on the mainland. Why not just let us do what's best for him?"

"We won't give our consent."

"I'm sorry to hear that, but I'm afraid the operation will have to go forward anyhow. Now let me be very frank. If you refuse, it will be necessary for security to come and get Geoffrey, and take you into custody if you resist. You can imagine for yourselves how much easier it will be for Geoffrey if you cooperate."

Geoffrey came back from the operating room with a little ceramic knob on his head. A wire led from the knob to a metal box with a pushbutton, which Geoffrey had been told to keep in his shirt pocket. When he pushed the button, the voices went away. He pushed the button all the time, and the children in his class called him "Boxhead."

**7** Among the early victims of McNulty's Disease in its original outbreak on CV were two passengers, Julie Prescott and John Stevens, who later married and had a daughter, Kimberly Anne. Stevens, not born under that name, was a former professional assassin who now called himself Robert Ames. Early in 2005 they went to England, where they had an unsatisfactory experience with a private school in Oxford; then to France, and finally to Italy.

In Frascati they found an American school where Kim seemed to get along a little better. The town was on the northern slope of the Alban Hills, high enough to be clear of the Roman smog, and expensive enough to be free of street crime. They lived in a hotel for a few weeks, then found a villa for lease; it needed extensive repairs, but had a fine view of the Campagna, and they could get to the Stazione Centrale in twenty minutes.

By gate-crashing embassy receptions and exerting his charm to the fullest, Stevens quickly made the acquaintance of the international set in Rome. One of them was a credulous young contessa named Isabella Giucci, with whom Stevens had a discreet affair, and who introduced him in turn to her titled friends as well as to a group of new-moneyed people who were happy to accept a vaguely aristocratic foreigner. Stevens called himself Peter Kauffman now and usually claimed to be Swiss. He spoke Italian with a French accent, which his new friends found charming.

Julie, who did not care for large gatherings, rented a studio near the Pincio and began to work in holoprints. Gradually she became part of a group of Roman painters and art dealers, and they saw a little less of each other.

In October, during a heat-wave, brown dust was blowing over from Africa, tinting the heavy air the color of cigarettes in a toilet bowl; Rome was insupportable, and even in the Hills the temperature at noon was over a hundred. The villa was air-conditioned, but the heat and the apocalyptic sky made Stevens restless. Late one night he got out of bed without waking Julie, went into the living room and turned on a popular talk show. The host was saying, "Professor Palladino, your theory as I understand it is a rather breathtaking one. In effect, you say that money is unnecessary, am I correct?"

Palladino, a bald brown man in his fifties, nodded and smiled. He spoke with a slight Calabrian accent. "Correct. Money is unnecessary in the modern world, but, let me say, not only unnecessary but harmful. Great accumulations of money give their possessors great power, which they use to harm us and distort our lives. With money one can make more money, and so on, whether or not one contributes anything to the lives of other people, and the result is that in this country almost ninety percent of the so-called wealth is owned by seven percent of the people. This is a familiar story, no one disputes it; the only question has always been, how can we remedy the situation? Well, the answer is very simple.

If there were no money, these great accumulations of wealth could not exist."

"Professor Palladino, forgive me, but I find these ideas very strange and I'm a bit confused. Let me ask you a few questions which you may find very elementary."

Palladino nodded, smiled. "With pleasure."

"Well, in the first place, then, let me ask, if there were no money, how would we get the things we want? By barter?"

"No, not by barter. In the moneyless society all goods will be free."

"They will be free? Everything?"

"Certainly. They will be distributed in just the same way, but there will be no payment. You will go to the food store, for instance, take a chicken, some eggs, milk and corn meal or whatever you need, and go home."

"Eh," said the host, and laughed. "That's very nice, but let's imagine that I'm the farmer who grows the chicken you have just put in your basket. Why should I put the chicken in the store for you to take?"

"Do you like to grow chickens?"

"I myself?"

"No, the farmer."

"Well, I suppose he must like to do it, or he would be doing something else. But why should he give the chickens away?"

"Why not? Whatever he himself wants is also free. You know, it is a myth that people work only for money. How many people are there in this country who want to be farmers but who have been driven off the land by the agricultural corporations? Do you imagine that if they could go back to the land and live without want, they would refuse because no one would pay them in money?"

"I see. But in fact, aren't there some jobs that nobody wants to do?"

"Would you be kind enough to name them?"

"Well . . ." The host gestured helplessly. "You know . . . sanitation and so forth."

"Sanitation is a worthy occupation," said Palladino. "To make things clean, what could be better? But you want to suggest that nobody likes dealing with dirty things, with ordures for instance. You assume that everyone would prefer to put on a collar and work in an office. But I think this is an unfounded assumption. I know some very happy people who clean cesspools, and I know some very unhappy people who work in offices."

"Ha, ha! But, for the sake of argument, wouldn't you admit that there are some jobs that nobody would do unless they were paid?"

"I don't think we know whether there are such jobs or not. Suppose we investigate carefully, and we find that in fact there are a few things that nobody wants to do. In the moneyless society, if they are necessary things, we will take turns doing them, because they must be done. But we may find that they are not necessary. Think of the cashier in the food store, and the bookkeeper, and the accountant who has to make sure all the numbers are in balance. This is not useful work. In the moneyless society those people will be liberated to perform tasks that are useful and pleasant."

"And if they don't choose to work at all?"

"How many people are there who really like to be idle? Do you?"

"I? No, but there are others—"

"Forgive me, I don't think so. There are young people who are idle because there is no work for them and they have not been trained to do anything useful. They are idle because they have no choice. Even most rich people are not idle. They are active in social and charitable organizations, in politics, or in professions and business. They are very busy people, and why? Because they like being busy, and they would hate being idle."

Stevens was amused and interested. He had met other eccentrics of this kind, people who could defend an apparently nonsensical position so logically that they left their questioners gasping and wordless. There had been a man in Oslo, for instance, who could prove absolutely that the Earth was flat. Then there were the cult leaders who talked solemnly about "energy" and "higher thought." There was a great deal of money in these enterprises, and the best part of it was that it was all legal; there was no law against taking money in exchange for nonsense.

A day or two later, passing a lecture hall near the Piazza Cola di Rienzo, he saw a poster on a board outside:

LIVE WITHOUT MONEY!
Free lecture by the renowned scholar, Professor Edgar Palladino.
Contributions accepted.

The lecture was at eleven, and it was almost that now. Suspecting a meaningful coincidence, Stevens followed a few shabbily dressed people into the lobby, where he found a young woman at a card table under a larger version of the same poster. On the card table was a pile of pamphlets, a stack of cards, and a box with some currency in it.

Stevens said, "Good morning. How much is the contribution?"

"Just whatever you like, Signor." She had a nice smile, and her figure was good. Stevens decided to be generous, and dropped five hundred new lire in the box.

"Thank you, Signor. The lecture is about to begin, but will you be kind enough to fill out one of these cards afterward? And please accept this little pamphlet."

Stevens took the card and pamphlet and left with a bow. Inside the lecture hall, about forty people were sitting in scattered clumps. Evidently the idea of living without money was not attractive to many. He had an impulse to leave, but suppressed it when a young man walked onto the platform. "Gentlemen and ladies, welcome. Today you are going to hear the most astounding message of the age, a message that will transform your lives. But first let me introduce myself. I am Bruno Colmari, a factory worker's son born exactly here, in Rome. Two years ago, in Milan, I met Professor Edgar Palladino, the distinguished scholar who will address you today. I listened to him speak, and realized that he alone has the solutions we are all seeking. Professor Palladino was awarded his doctorate of philosophy in Padua in nineteen eighty-five, and he has taught and lectured in Naples, Paris, and many other world capitals. He is the author of *The Optimal Society* and many other distinguished works of scholarship. Today he comes to tell you how you can transform your lives. Please welcome Professor Edgar Palladino!"

Following his cue, there was a polite scattering of applause. Palladino, in an ill-fitting brown suit, walked out from the wing. He shook hands with Colmari, who retired. Palladino took a determined stance behind the lectern. He began to speak in a voice so low that Stevens had to strain to hear.

"My good friends, it is a pleasure to see you here today. You are few in number, but as Edward Young said, the mountains are made of grains of sand. Now let me prepare you a little for what you are about to hear. You will find it surprising at first, but please listen with an open mind. It is very simple: you can live without money. How? By cooperating with others who also want to live without money. That's all that is necessary. As things now stand, we have collectively agreed to pretend that we need money, a fictitious medium of exchange. What is it? It is not even plastic coins or paper any more, things worthless in themselves, it is numbers in the memories of computers. And these numbers rule our lives and enable others to become rich at our expense. Now let us suppose that we all collectively agree to stop pretending that we need money. What will the consequences be?

"Let's imagine that in a certain town the people discover one day that all the money has disappeared. Behold!" He looked around with a comical grimace. "It has gone, no one knows where! What is to be done? The people come together to discuss the matter. One says, 'Well, if there is no more money, we must use barter. I will bring my cow to market, and my vegetables, and trade them for whatever I need, and you, my friend the shoemaker, will barter your shoes.'"

He paused and looked around again. "The shoemaker says, 'That sounds very well, but how am I going to barter a pair of shoes for a cow?'"

"'Simple,' says the farmer. 'You, my friend the butcher, will slaughter the cow and cut it up into roasts and steaks, keeping some for your trouble, and with one or two of these good pieces of meat I will purchase the shoes.'

"And they all agree that this is a good plan, but then the tractor dealer says, 'For myself, I see a little difficulty. One of my tractors is worth more than any cow, and even if I took ten cows in payment, that would be more meat than I could eat in a year. What am I to do with all this meat? Before I can trade it for things I want, it will spoil.' And the schoolmaster says, 'Frankly, I don't see how I am to be paid for the work I do. The shoemaker's children are all grown; he will not give me shoes, and the tractor dealer will not give me a tractor. If he did, what would I do with it?'

"So they all begin to see that the problem is not so simple as it first appeared. Then someone says, 'Perhaps we are going about it the wrong way. We are talking about a substitute for money—barter, which is inconvenient and unwieldy. But what if we don't need any substitute for money? Each of us produces something that is of use to others. The farmer raises cows and vegetables, the tanner tans hides, the shoemaker makes shoes, the tractor dealer distributes tractors, the schoolmaster educates our children. Let us agree to give away the things we produce to anyone who asks for them. Then the farmer will have his tractor, the schoolmaster will have his shoes, the shoemaker will have bread—in short, everything will be exactly as before, except that we will have done it all without money.' "

At the end of the lecture Palladino called for questions. There were only two, the same ones that the holo interviewer had raised; Palladino answered them with patience and humor, but the audience, when it straggled out, did not look deeply impressed.

Evidently Palladino's organization was just getting started; it was small, badly financed, and amateurish. At the moment he was merely one crackpot among many; later he might be a very successful guru. The opportunity was attractive; Stevens decided to make a modest investment.

After the next lecture, he approached the young woman behind the card table and offered her a bundle of notes which he had obtained earlier from the bank. "I would like to make a small contribution," he said. "I'm sorry it isn't more."

The woman counted the money with a smile of delight. "Oh, this is wonderful of you, Signor—"

"Peter Kauffman," said Stevens. "And you?"

"My name is Maria Orsi, Signor Kauffman. I'm happy to make your acquaintance." She offered her hand. "Now let me write you a receipt. You know, Professor Palladino has nothing. Really, he is like a medieval saint. A few friends try to see that he has something in his pockets, but he gives it all away."

"Well, it's honorable for a philosopher to be poor, but

there is a paradox involved. It will take money to establish the moneyless society."

"That's so true. I'm glad you understand. Perhaps, Signor Kauffman, you would like to come to one of our little private meetings? Just a few of the Professor's closest friends."

"I should be delighted."

**8** Randy Geller and Yvonne Barlow lived in a comfortable apartment in the perm section of CV. Perm was laid out almost like a small town; the corridors had street names, and there was a park and a town square. A lively group of young people circulated in the neighborhood, and somebody threw a party every weekend.

The Ottenburgs were one of the couples Geller and Barlow saw frequently. Steve was an engineer who worked in the machine shop, and Andrea was a kindergarten teacher. One evening at a party Geller took Andrea aside and said, "Hey, how's it going?"

"Not too bad. How about you?"

"Could be worse. Listen, can you get me some spray paint, preferably green?"

"Sure. One can?"

"No, say about twenty?"

"Twenty cans? What are you going to do with it?"

"A special project. Very hush-hush."

She looked at him seriously. "All right. I'll bring it home a few cans at a time, all right?"

"Sure. And maybe some green markers—twenty or thirty?"

"Okay. Sure you don't want to tell me what you're up to?"

"If you don't know, you can't tell. Do you have to sign requisitions or anything?"

"I'm supposed to, but everybody just takes it from the storeroom."

"That's fine."

The next night, after Yvonne and the child were asleep, he got up quietly and dressed in slacks, tennis shoes and a sweatshirt. He got a spray can out of the closet and put it in the sweatshirt pocket. He left without waking Yvonne, went out the back way into the service alley and emerged into the main street a block away. Only the nightlights were on, but the dim blue light was enough to make out the spy-eyes and their wiring scabbed to the walls near the ceiling—little fisheye lenses, one about every fifty feet. Geller did a dry run and timed it; it took him forty seconds to do the six hundred feet between Pacific and Oak. Were the spy-eyes tracking him, even in this dim light? More likely they were infrared sensitive, but that would give a blurred image anyhow.

The echo of his footsteps died away. The street was still empty; nobody had come out to see what he was up to. Geller took the spray can out of his pocket and wrote on the wall, "THE GREEN HORNET STRIKES." He aimed the spray at the nearest lens. After a couple of seconds an alarm bell began to ring. Geller sprayed that, too, and after a moment it stopped. He raced along the street, hitting one lens after another. Then another alarm bell. He dropped the spray can in a trash receptacle and went home.

"You did that, didn't you?" Yvonne asked.

"Yup."

"What's this Green Hornet supposed to be?"

"I don't know, a comix hero, maybe. It's a story my dad used to tell when he thought I wasn't listening. This first-grade teacher happens to notice one day there's a puddle of pee in the cloakroom. So she calls all the kids together, and she tells them she's going to turn out the lights and leave the room for five minutes. While she's gone, whoever made the puddle is supposed to mop it up, and that'll be the end of it, okay? So she goes and comes back, and now there are *two* puddles of pee in the cloakroom, and a note that says, 'The Green Hornet strikes again.'"

In the lab, he concocted a colorless hygroscopic goo that would turn liquid and green in about three hours. At five o'clock in the morning, when the snack bar was still dark, he went in, climbed on a table with his bucket, and painted goo in a stripe six inches wide and five feet long at the top of the end wall. At breakfast three hours later, he was rewarded by the sound of laughter and cheering. The green goo, appearing out of nowhere, was dripping in slow gouts down the wall. There were shouts of "The Green Hornet!" and more cheers.

During the next few days Geller left spray cans and green markers in inconspicuous places throughout the Main Deck. By Friday evening they were all gone.

After dinner on Tuesday, the face of Captain MacDonald Trilling appeared in all the holos. He was the chief of the Wackenhuts, the contract security people. "You know," he said with his meaningless smile, "we have talked before about keeping CV a pleasant place for all of us to live. Well, what does that mean, a pleasant place to live? I suppose it means a place where we can all be comfortable and get everything we need. And it means a place where we can have stimulating experiences. By that I mean all kinds of things—social meetings, parties, entertainments, and so on. Well, lately we've been having a new kind of entertainment—the Green Hornet.

"I want to talk to you about that. Where do we draw the line between things that are entertaining and things that are dangerous? The Green Hornet, whoever he or she may be, has been doing some things that endanger all of us. For instance, blinding the security cameras in the corridors. That's just a nuisance, in the sense that it takes somebody's time to clean the paint off, but what if they ruined the lenses? Then there would be no way to detect and punish crime in the corridors. And believe me, it's happened before. Violent assault, rape—do you want that to happen again? Talk to your friends. If you know anybody who is involved in these games, see if you can explain to them what they're risking. That's all. Have a good evening."

Security people came and took away all the green markers in storerooms, the green paint, green tape, green construction paper. Two days later, the camera lenses in the corridors were sprayed with blue paint. On the wall was smeared, THE BLUE HORNET STRIKES AGAIN!

At the staff meeting the next day Melanie Kurtz said,

"I'm absolutely opposed to any room searches or anything of that kind. If we create an oppressive atmosphere for the grownups, it can't help affecting the children."

"Which ones are the children?" Cunningham wanted to know.

"Well, they're behaving childishly, of course. It's probably just a few people, not more than a dozen or so out of the whole detainee population. Teenagers, maybe. But the rest of the detainees seem to be enjoying it. If we do anything of a disciplinary or retaliatory nature, we're going to see some resentment."

"We can't let this go on. What do you suggest, Melanie?"

"Let them have their fun. They'll get tired of it."

Two Wackenhut guards, Ronald Guest and Daryl Singlaub, entering the cafeteria where they usually had their lunch, heard a peculiar noise behind them: first a single "Oink," barely audible, then a low-voiced chorus. "Oink. Oink. Oink." When they turned around, the noises stopped; the diners looked at them innocently. As soon as they started walking again, the noises resumed.

Singlaub turned and said, "Look, people, we're just doing our job. How about a little courtesy?"

No one replied. When they went to the steam table, the chorus resumed. The unsmiling food handler gave them their dishes; one of them tipped and spilled gravy on Guest's hand.

Guest wiped his hand with a paper napkin. The two young men took their trays to a table against the wall where they could see the length of the room, but as soon as they sat down, from left and right came the chorus of "Oink." They stood it for five minutes, then got up and walked out, pursued by a chorus of "Oink" that grew louder and louder.

"Some of you," Trilling's voice said on the loudspeakers, "have been making insulting noises to our security people. You must realize—"

In the mall and the corridors, oinking sounds were heard, almost drowning out his voice.

"—as sensitive to this kind of abuse as you would be yourselves. All we're asking is a little cooperation and courtesy. We have to work this out together. Ask yourselves—"

"Oink. Oink. Oink."

"—this were happening to you. I know that when you think it over—"

"Oink. Oink. Oink."

"Thank you."

Trilling called in the chairperson of the Detainee Council, the body that theoretically made and enforced those rules for detainees that were not made administratively from above. The chairperson was a ruddy man in his sixties named Davidson. "What do you want me to do, tell them not to say 'Oink'? They want to say 'Oink,' they'll say it."

"No, no, Mr. Davidson, I just want to consult with you and get your suggestions. What can we do to improve relations with the detainees?"

"The prisoners, you mean."

"No, you're not *prisoners*—I mean, you're not here because of any crime."

"You think that makes it *better*?"

"If that's your attitude—"

"Oink," said Davidson.

Keeping a low profile, Trilling withdrew his people from routine patrols and ordered them to take their meals in a cafeteria that had been made off-limits to detainees. The result was an increase in graffiti. Scurrilous poems began to appear on the walls. One of them went:

> A certain policeman named Trilling
> Would do anything for a shilling.
>    When Owen said, "Mac,
>    Kindly lie on your back,"
> He answered, "Why, madam, I'm willing."

Trilling sent out night crews to clean the walls, and bided his time. One afternoon there was a food fight in a cafeteria, and the manager phoned for assistance. Trilling refused to send anyone, and he persuaded the Maintenance director not to let his people clean up the room. After two days the detainees cleaned it up themselves. Then things went a little better, but morale among the Wackenhuts was not what it had been.

**9** Christmas cards and packages for Dr. Owen had been piling up in her secretary's office for a week—hundreds of them; at least a tenth of the detainee families on CV must have given her something, in addition to the staff. That was heartening, and it was evidence that the morale problems were being dealt with. On Christmas morning Corcoran said, "Dr. Owen, your presents have all been through X-ray. Would you like me to open them now?"

"Yes, that would be fine. Keep a list, of course."

Half an hour later he called again. "Doctor, I think you should see this." On his desk was an opened package and a strip of heavy plastic about the size of a ruler. Both were smeared with some green substance, and there were splatters on the desk, the keyboard, the wall, and Corcoran himself; there was even a faint green smear on the holo pickup, like a film of algae.

"My goodness, Jim, are you hurt? What is that?"

"My guess is green jello," Corcoran said. "This"—he touched the strip of plastic—"was folded up inside like a flat spring. It didn't show on the X-ray, of course."

"Let me see the wrapping."

Corcoran held it up. It was one of the standard Christmas wraps available in the stores—green, with little Santa Clauses and reindeer.

"Of course I don't want you to open any more," Owen said. "I'm terribly sorry this has happened."

"It could have been something corrosive, or poisonous," Corcoran said. His voice shook a little.

"Well, just to make sure, I think you'd better wash thoroughly, and change your clothes, don't you? And call security to pick up the rest of the presents. Take the day off, Jim, and try to have a merry Christmas."

The exploding present had been meant for her, of course; the donor had not known that Corcoran would open it instead. Probably there were others like it somewhere in the stack; possibly there was something worse.

What a cowardly thing to do; how unfair and contemptible!

"Mitzi," she said to the computer, "someone on CV has been playing jokes of a kind calculated to disrupt our routines and make it difficult for us to carry on our work. Can you interpret personality profiles of the detainees in order to determine who would be most likely to do such a thing?"

"Can you explain the jokes, Dr. Owen?"

"He paints over the lenses of closed-circuit vision cameras, using green paint, and writes on the wall, 'The Green Hornet Strikes Again.' We believe other people have begun copying him, but there was one person who began it."

"Can you explain 'The Green Hornet Strikes Again'?"

"I believe it's a reference to an old radio program dealing with a masked hero called the Green Hornet."

"What does a masked hero do, Dr. Owen?"

"He conceals his identity and pops up in unexpected places to capture criminals and rescue innocent people."

"Does this imply that the person you are looking for regards the non-detainees as criminals, and the detainees as innocent people who should be rescued?"

"Yes, I think so. The campaign is effective because people think it's humorous. He's making fun of us, in fact, and that diminishes our authority."

"I won't ask you to explain humor, Dr. Owen, but can you say how this campaign differs from other kinds of humor?"

"It's a little offbeat, I'd say."

"Unusual, that is?"

"Yes."

"Would you say that the person you are looking for shows an unusual degree of hostility toward the non-detainees?"

"Yes, certainly."

"And that he would be likely to have expressed it before in an offbeat fashion?"

"That seems likely."

"One moment. In the scores of Thematic Appercep-tion Tests of current detainees I find the following comment or a similar one on seventeen cases: 'Subject's narratives show attempted humor masking hostility toward the experimenter.'"

"Who are these detainees? Put them on the flatscreen."

The names appeared in alphabetical order: Abrams, Alfred R.; Denmore, Tina Marie; Geller, Randall . . .

"Geller!" she said. At that moment she really knew,

but she had to make sure. "What do you have on the TATs, Mitzi—transcripts, voice recordings?"

"I have complete voice recordings."

"Let me hear Geller's."

There was a scraping sound, then a voice. "Hello, Mr. Geller. Feeling all right today?"

"Peachy."

"Fine. Just sit down there at the terminal, if you would. Now this morning I'm going to show you some pictures, and I want you to look at them and make up a story about each one. Here's the first picture."

A long silence followed. "Just anything that comes to mind," said the voice.

"Okay. You want me to just say anything that comes to my mind, right?"

"That's right. Just make up a story."

"Well, this kid, his name is Ralph, he lives in Michigan with his father and his stepmother. The old man is okay, but he drinks a lot and when he drinks he likes to set fire to schoolhouses, so you can imagine the home life is not too great."

Owen watched her hands curl into fists.

"Now the stepmother, Imogene, is a frustrated ballet dancer who keeps leaping around the house all day in her tutu. The only thing the kid has going for him is his dog, Spot. They call him Spot because he loses his bladder control whenever he sits on the furniture. Well, one day in the early summer, a Wednesday, Ralph takes good old Spot out for a walk in the woods. Now Spot is blind in one eye, but he's a hell of a hunter, and when he sees a rabbit in the bushes he takes off and he's gone. The rabbit gets on his blind side and runs away, but Spot won't give up, and the kid is running after him, yelling, 'Pot! Pot!' Kid can't say his S's, so he's yelling, 'Pot! Pot!'"

Owen said, "That's enough, Mitzi. Thank you." She sat for a while holding her hands quite still on the desk, but her anger did not abate.

She knew, of course, what Geller was up to. He was trying to make CV ungovernable, in the hope that the detainees would be discharged either at Manila or at some later port of call. Her impulse was to punish him, and she thought of incarceration, posting to the experimental section, public humiliation . . . but that was emotion, not logic. What was best to be done? Once she had asked the question, the answer was clear.

Three weeks later CV docked at Manila after midnight. At four o'clock three security people entered Geller and Barlow's bedroom and turned on the light.

Geller sat up. "Now what?"

"Get up and get dressed, please," said the tallest of the three. "Dress the child, too, and pack anything you want to take with you. You're leaving CV."

Dizzy with sleep, Geller looked at the bedside clock. "Good Christ, it's four o'clock in the morning. Can't it wait?"

"Shut up, Randy," said Yvonne. She was out of bed already, reaching for her robe.

"We'll wait in the living room," said the security man. "Please don't take more than twenty minutes, and don't make any unnecessary noise." The three of them left the room.

Yvonne did the packing while Geller got Geoffrey up

and dressed him. "All ready?" said the spokesman. "Are those all your bags?"

"We had to leave some stuff behind."

"It will be packed and sent after you. Come on now, and please be very quiet."

"Can you explain why we're being hustled out in the middle of the night?"

"Orders."

"Oh. Why didn't I think of that?"

They passed through the perm checkpoint and walked all the way up G corridor to the forward lobby. The security people did not offer to help them with the luggage. Another security person checked them out. At the bottom of the gangway a limousine with closed curtains was waiting. "The driver will take you to the airport," said the spokesman. "Tickets to San Francisco will be waiting at the Pan Am desk." Then two security people held them while a third took Geoffrey out of Yvonne's arms. Both parents struggled, and Barlow got in one good kick, but the Wacks wrestled them both to the ground and sprayed them with something. Then the Wacks loaded them into the limousine. They were already feeling drowsy when it pulled away toward the darkness.

"And now—the President of the United States!"

The jowly face of President Draffy appeared in the holos. "My fellow citizens," he said, "as you know, for the past eighteen months we have been implementing a program for the monitoring of career criminals, utilizing a transponder device enclosed in an unbreakable brace-let or anklet, such that the location of each monitoree can be determined at all times. This procedure has resulted in a *dramatic drop* in crime rates on the streets of our cities, and there has been a corresponding *decline* in our prison populations.

"If a burglar enters your home, for instance, we know where he is and we know he has no right to be there. If somebody snatches your purse and runs, we know who he is and we can follow him wherever he goes.

"This system has been so successful that we have been urged to extend it to all citizens. I am glad to be able to tell you tonight that with bipartisan support, the joint Congressional committee has worked out a compromise version of the Citizen Monitoring and Identification Act, and it is likely to become law during this session.

"This will mean enormous benefits in security and safety for all of us! If you are lost in the wilderness during a camping trip, or if you have an accident, you can be located swiftly and surely. If your child wanders away and is lost, or if she is lured into a vehicle by a sex offender, or into his house, we can find her.

"It has been charged by a few dissidents that this system will be used for excessive governmental control, but I point out tonight to those so-called dissidents that the law protects everyone equally, and that a person who *doesn't* break the law has nothing to fear. Law-abiding citizens will be safer than they ever have been; criminals will be swiftly apprehended and punished. When this law is implemented, we will all sleep sounder in our beds. Thank you and good night."

"Well, you're definitely pregnant," the doctor said. "How do you feel about that?"

The patient blushed. "I think it's wonderful."

"Okay, then there's one more procedure we need to do." He tapped a key, handed her the pink sheet that came out. "Take this down to Radiology Labs on the first floor."

"What is it?"

"Just a routine procedure."

She found Radiology and handed the slip to the receptionist, who gave her a form to fill out. After a long wait, a nurse led her into a room with some kind of machine in it: two wooden uprights with a black metal disk that moved on tracks between them. The nurse said, "Stand up on the platform." She pressed a control; the disk moved down an inch or two. "Put your tummy right up against it."

The disk was cold through her summer dress. The nurse pressed another button; a red light blinked. "Okay, that's all." She waited until the patient stepped off the platform, then pressed the controls again. The disk whined up its tracks and disappeared behind the shield at the top. Then there was a crackling sound and a funny smell. "What was that for?" the patient asked.

"Just to make sure your baby wasn't carrying a McNulty's parasite. If there was one in there, it's gone now."

For the love of money is the root of all evil:
which while some coveted after, they have
erred from the faith, and pierced themselves
through with many sorrows.

i TIMOTHY, 6:10

**10** On days when it was possible to breathe
without a mask, Stevens walked the
streets of Rome, looking at people with a new curiosity.
Here among the crowds of African and Asian mendi-
cants were petty shopkeepers, a few artisans plying their
trades, office workers going to their anonymous jobs: all
of them, presumably, making some contribution in
return for which they were fed and housed. But there
were others who contributed nothing, and Stevens himself was one of these. What if he had grown up in a world
where the use of violence had become impossible—the
world which he saw taking shape around him at this
moment? It could have happened, if he had been born
only thirty years later. What would that man have been
like? He could not answer the question, and he could not
leave it alone. He had done what he had to do, yes, he
still believed that, but if he had not had to do it, what

would he have done instead? Suppose someone had said to him, you will be fed and housed in comfort, you don't need to worry about that; now what will you do with your life?

What if Palladino's insane dream came true? The farmers would give away their crops, the manufacturers their machines, the workers their labor. And he himself, would he be merely a social parasite, taking everything and giving nothing? Impossible.

He remembered his infatuation with poetry at seventeen. Years ago he had tried to translate Villon into English, God knows why. The lines came back to him now:

> In the thirtieth year of my age
> When I had drunk down all my shames
> Neither an utter fool nor quite a sage
> Notwithstanding all the pains
> Thibault d'Aussigny gave me for my diet
> Bishop he may be, for all his gains
> Say he is mine and I'll deny it
> He is neither my bishop nor my lord
> Nothing he gave me but the scraps and rind
> I owe him neither cross nor sword
> I am not his villein nor his hind
> On a small loaf all year I dined
> And had cold water for my wine
> Open or stingy, he remained unkind
> May God be to him as he was to me

He had been attracted to Villon, no doubt, because of that settled resentment, the feeling of being an outcast, his hand against every man: but Villon had been nothing if not an unsuccessful thief.

This Thibault d'Aussigny of whom Villon complained was the Bishop of Orléans who had put him in prison, perhaps for stealing a votive lamp from a church, a crime of small account except that it might have been treated as sacrilege.

Say, then, was Villon's misery his own fault or that of the world around him? In a better world, would he have had enough to eat without stealing—and would he then have written better or worse poetry?

That night, after the child was asleep, he found Villon's verses in the net and printed them out. One stanza caught his eye:

> *Je congnois pourpoint au colet,*
> *Je congnois le moyne a la gonne,*
> *Je congnois le maistre au varlet,*
> *Je congnois au voille la nonne,*
> *Je congnois quant pipeur jargonne,*
> *Je congnois folz nourris de cresmes,*
> *Je congnois le vin a la tonne,*
> *Je congnois tout, fors que moy mesmes.*

Literally, it was something like, "I know the doublet by its hem, I know the monk by his habit. I know the master by the man, I know the nun by her veil. I know when a conman talks jargon, I know fools fed on creams. I know wine by the barrel, I know everything except myself."

If the poet were alive tonight, and if he were an English speaker, what would he write? Some of his rhymes were forced, for instance "cresmes" and "moy mesmes": he would not have done that if the language had given him a better choice. After a while he thought he saw some others that the poet might have liked. He wrote, and crossed out, and in an hour he had:

> I know the longbow by its wood,
> I know the wagon by its wheel.
> I know the hangman by his hood,
> I know the horseman by his heel.
> I know the sharper by his spiel,
> I know the bottles on the shelf.
> I know the swordsman by his steel,
> I know everything except myself.

The more he read about Villon the more deeply interested he grew. As a young scholar, Villon had actually been proposed for a benefice and might have died a bishop; but then, as Wyndham Lewis said, "The Church would have gained a rascal and poetry would have lost a prince." At the age of thirty-two he was arrested for a crime of which he was more or less innocent, tortured, and condemned to be "hanged and strangled." On appeal, since the case was weak but Villon's odor was strong, his sentence was commuted to ten years' exile from Paris. That was the last anyone ever heard of him. Although he wrote, in *The Debate of the Heart and Body of Villon,* that the fault was in his stars, it was certainly his character and not mere circumstance that made him a criminal. He might have become a prelate, like many of his class at the University of Paris; instead, he chose poverty, crime, and poetry.

**11** Stevens looked up Palladino in the net and found two books, *The Optimal Society* and *The Myth of Money,* both in Italian. As he had expected, there were not many reviews, and none by people whose names he had seen before. The books were under copyright; he paid the fees and downloaded them. Over the weekend he read them both; they were witty and surprisingly lucid, like the man himself. There was an English translation of *The Optimal Society;* Stevens sampled that too, and found it badly done.

Palladino was staying with friends in a vast shabby apartment near the river. When Stevens arrived at the appointed hour, he found the professor seated at a tea table with Maria Orsi and four others: Bruno Colmari, the young man who had introduced Palladino at the lectures, an elderly couple named Lanciani who were the owners of the apartment, and a blond middle-aged woman named Carla della Seta.

Palladino welcomed him effusively. "My dear young friend, come in. You have given us money, now let us give you tea."

"Since the money is worthless," Stevens could not help saying, "I am getting the better of the bargain."

Palladino laughed. "Quite true! When you came in, we

were just talking about this worthless money that we must have. You know, the goldsmiths used to keep gold on deposit for their customers and issue receipts for it, which the customers could use to pay their debts, and these receipts circulated like currency.

"Well, the goldsmiths, who were now bankers whether they wanted to be or not, discovered that in any given period only a certain percentage of these receipts would be presented for payment; therefore they could issue more receipts, which would also circulate like currency even though there was no gold to back them, and by loaning these receipts they could gain interest on this imaginary gold. And so you see that all the weight of modern finance rests on a fantasy!

"Every bank today loans more money than it actually has, and each time this imaginary money is deposited in another bank, it generates still more imaginary money. Well, all money is imaginary now, because there is nothing to back it. You cannot go to a bank or to a state treasury and redeem your money for gold or anything of value; but everyone accepts the imaginary money and therefore it is as good as if it were real. We agree to pretend that it exists, you see, and so the world goes round and everyone is happy, except those who have no money.

"What if we gave everyone some of this imaginary money? It costs nothing to make it, since it does not exist; but then, we say, there would be too much money, and since everyone would want to spend it, the prices of goods would be driven up. Yes, and we also say that we must have new markets for the goods we produce. Only in a world where imaginary things are treated as real could we believe these two contradictory things at once."

"But, Professor," said Stevens, "even if money is imaginary, isn't it true that goods are real and that if there are fewer goods than people who want to buy them, the prices will go up?"

"My dear friend, you are still thinking in terms of money. Without money, there will be no prices."

"Very good, but then how do we decide who gets my chicken, if there are five who want it?"

Palladino beamed. "Let us have a demonstration. Let each of us put something of value on the table. Not money, and not anything of great value—just some trifle, a thing we would be willing to give away to a friend." He looked in his pockets. "I don't seem to have anything. Wait, here is a nail-clipper. That will do very well." He dropped it on the table. Maria contributed a little mirror, Bruno a packet of tissues, Signora della Seta a pencil, the two Lancianis respectively a bottle of scent and a key-chain without the keys. Stevens added his Swiss Army knife.

"Very good!" said Palladino. "Now let us say that each of us desires each of these things. But there is only one of each thing, and there are seven of us. And we have no money! What can we do? First we write our names on slips of paper." He wrote on a pad, tore off a piece and folded it, passed the pad around. "Now, dear Rosa, may we use this bowl? Excellent." He put the folded slips in the bowl. "Maria, will you be kind enough to draw? We will draw first for the nail-clipper."

Maria unfolded the slip. "Signor Kauffman." Next the tissues, which Palladino got; the scent bottle, Bruno;

Signor Lanciani got his own key-chain. Maria got the knife. The pencil went to Signora della Seta and Signora Lanciani got the mirror.

"Now it is a rule of these demonstrations," said Palladino jovially, "that we do not give our prizes back. Another time we may offer them again and get something else instead. But we see now, do we not, that without the use of money we can decide who is to have something each of us wants. And if we are sometimes disappointed, well, we have been disappointed before. Is your question answered?" he said to Stevens.

"Yes, and I see that there are other ways, too—a waiting list, for example."

"Of course, and another way is for me to give you something just because I like you more than I like Maria. These are imperfect ways, but the money way is imperfect too, I think. Don't you agree?"

"I do, indeed," said Stevens gravely. "But there is something else that disturbs me. In the moneyless society, the farmer will contribute his cows and grain, the shoemaker his shoes, and so on, and everything will come out even. But what will I contribute?"

"What can you do? What have you done before?"

"Nothing very useful. I have invested in stocks and in precious metals. I wrote a little poetry when I was young."

Palladino smiled. "Then you will contribute your poetry."

Stevens said, "Forgive me, but I can't believe my poetry would be worth all those tractors and shoes."

Palladino leaned forward. "That is exactly the point. We don't weigh one thing against another, we don't assign prices or numbers. If your poetry is·all you have to give, you give it. Even if you have nothing to give—if you are old and infirm, let's say—still there are enough things to go around. You can have meat, you can have shoes. Why not? There is enough."

After the last lecture, when Palladino was about to leave for Naples, Stevens said to him, "Professor, perhaps while you are gone I could undertake a little organization here in Rome, collect some money, distribute pamphlets and so on?"

"My dear friend, I would be very grateful. Bruno and Maria do what they can, but there is never enough time."

"And it also occurred to me, if it would not be an impertinence, I would like to translate some of your works into English and French."

"Marvelous! Yes, by all means!" Palladino got up to embrace him and sat back, beaming.

"And, of course, Professor, I would like something with your signature authorizing me to do these things."

"Of course, of course."

The problem was to create a cadre, a hard core of dedicated Palladinists who could then recruit others, and so on, making sure that one proof of dedication was to consist of generous contributions to the group. Stevens persuaded the Lancianis to hold weekly meetings at their apartment, where, first modestly and then with more confidence, he set forth his program.

He also began to talk about the moneyless society whenever he met his rich friends. "But that's fascinating!" said the dotty old Contessa di Corso. "Think of living without any money at all! I really would like to give him something, dear Peter. Who shall I write the check to?"

"Not a check, please. As a matter of principle, Palladino does not pay taxes. He accepts only cash, which he doesn't have to report."

"But they'll put him in jail, won't they?"

"He thinks he could write a very good book in jail."

Encouraged by the success of these trial balloons, during the next few months Stevens went to the introductory lectures of an Indian guru, a self-maximization program, and a New Age chiliastic organization, and enrolled in classes at all three. The exhortations were very wearing, particularly since he was getting three kinds at once. "Why are you doing this?" Julie asked.

"It's very interesting."

And, in fact, it was. The three groups had several things in common: a charismatic leader, an efficient and cynical leadership, and a hierarchical program designed to lead the converts, by means of larger and larger promises, into paying larger and larger fees. When the converts became sufficiently indoctrinated, they indoctrinated and trained new converts in their turn, and received a portion of the new fees as their share. By degrees it was made clear to the converts that the group was the most important thing in their lives. Great attention was paid to neat appearance and dress, positive emotions and enthusiasm. By every possible means the converts were bound together and isolated from nonbelievers. The enthusiasm was infectious: Stevens found himself in a state of continual nervous excitement, and had to resort to sleeping pills.

At the end of three months he believed he understood the dynamics of these groups sufficiently for his purposes, and he dropped out with relief. He had lost twenty pounds.

*12* One morning in the spring of that year, Robert S. Windom's desk computer said, "Call from Andrew Vick of Standing Wave Transportation, boss. He wants to speak to you personally."

"What the hell is Standing Wave?"

"Just a moment. Standing Wave Transportation, incorporated in Delaware, a subsidiary of Transport Systems, Ltd., a British corporation. President, Laurence Hawkins; Chief Executive Officer, Douglas De Angelo."

"Okay. Is that a new company? I never heard of it."

"Date of incorporation is January 21, 2005."

"Standard and Poor's rating?"

"Triple A."

"See if you can find anything about them in the net."

"Searching. An article in *Business Day,* March 23, 2005."

"Put it on."

The article came up in the flatscreen. Windom scanned it quickly; it wasn't much. ". . . intends to develop the so-called 'standing wave' system of instantaneous transportation based on the work of the Danish mathematician Olvard Torreson (*d.* 1989)."

What the hell. "Okay, Benji, put him on."

A face appeared in the tube, young, pale, brown-haired, rather attractive. "Mr. Windom, my name is Andrew Vick; I'm an assistant to Douglas De Angelo, the CEO of Standing Wave Transportation. We're interested in a feasibility study, and we'd like to know if your firm can devote a substantial amount of time to it beginning fairly soon."

"Let me find out. Benji, work schedule." The chart came up on the flatscreen. "I have a four-week window beginning on January third. Is that what you mean by a substantial amount of time?"

"I think it might be more like six months, but you would be the best judge of that."

Windom hesitated. "There are a few things we could put off, but I'd have to know more about it first."

"That's satisfactory. Would it be possible for you to come and talk to Mr. De Angelo sometime this week?"

"Yes, I suppose so. Let me turn you over to my secretary." He gave the call to the computer, then sat back a moment and thought. The computer said, "Nine-thirty June eighth, boss."

"Thanks."

"Don't mention it."

Windom, the head of the consulting firm that bore his name, was a red-haired, freckled man of forty-eight who liked cats, beer and jazz, in that order. He had been a project design supervisor with Martin Marietta until he began to feel peculiar about some of the work he was doing. The consulting firm he had founded after that was doing fairly well, although not as well as he sometimes pretended. Like other people in his profession, he worked himself too hard and sometimes felt depressed on Mondays.

He searched Torreson and got a little more. Eight years after the mathematician's death, his unpublished papers had been discovered in a library in Copenhagen. Among them was a solution of Schrödinger's wave equation which made it possible to transport an object instantaneously from one location to another. This so-called "uncivilized" solution had been known and ignored for years, but Torreson had added a hint of a way to make practical use of it. An international team of physicists and engineers had taken it to the point of laboratory demonstration. It sounded crazy, but it smelled like money, and besides, he was curious.

The reception room of Standing Wave Transportation in Newark was neat but very small. Precisely at nine-thirty, Windom was ushered into the office of Douglas De Angelo, a heavy-set man in his early fifties, with a smooth face and an easy smile. The office was also neat but small. De Angelo came around his desk to welcome the visitor, led him to a comfortable chair and sat down on the sofa opposite the coffee table. "Glad you could come, Mr. Windom. Some coffee?"

"Yes, please."

De Angelo poured from the silver thermos. "Cream and sugar?"

"No, black."

After a few social remarks, De Angelo said, "I suppose you know what SWT is."

"Just what's been on the net. It sounds like lunacy to me."

"Me too. I've just been handed this, and I don't understand how it works, but I've got people who say they do."

"Mr. De Angelo—"

"Make it Doug."

"Okay, Doug, my field is aerospace—that's the only kind of mass transportation there is anymore. I don't know a thing about rolling stock, if that's what you have in mind."

De Angelo looked pleased. "What made you say rolling stock?"

"Well, it's obvious that if you're going to zap something across lines of latitude, you have to compensate for the differences in rotational speed—unless you're breaking all the laws of physics, not just one or two."

"Good. You're right, and I think you may be the man for us. Let me just tell you generally what we're up against, so far as I understand it. The first thing we have to know is how many stations for a complete worldwide network, and where? The next thing—"

Windom leaned forward. "Wait a minute. What do you mean by a complete network? Major cities, or Bent Fork, Texas?"

"Major cities, but if the line passes through other places we'll do traffic projections. Okay? Next thing, design of the vehicles, one kind for passenger, one or two for freight. We need to know what constraints the vehicle design puts on the standing wave transport devices and vice versa. Then there's propulsion systems, then passenger and freight terminals, then warehousing and so on. We can't move on any of that until we have a basic concept that we know we're going to stick to. I'll give you copies of the patents before you leave, but first, I suppose you'd like to see a demonstration?"

"Yes, I would."

De Angelo took him to a small windowless room where a young woman was waiting. "Bob, this is LeAnne Bondy, she's our demonstrator."

Windom said hello, but he barely glanced at the woman; his attention was on the apparatus. It was on two glass-topped tables six feet apart: each was a metal cylinder about a foot long, horizontal on a black plastic stand, with a control board attached. A hinged cap on one end of each cylinder was open. Windom had expected to see cables, but there was only an ordinary electrical cord leading from each device to a baseboard outlet. He stooped to look inside the nearest cylinder: he saw metal rings, closely spaced, and a glimpse of wiring. "How much power does this thing use?"

"Ten watts. We could run it off penlight batteries."

Windom stooped further to look under the table. When he straightened up, De Angelo and Bondy were smiling. "Everybody does that," Bondy said. "We've had people feeling around for mirrors, and pipes hidden in the table legs. It doesn't make us mad, because it really does look like some kind of trick. But it isn't, it's real." She picked up a small glass paperweight from the table and handed it to Windom. "Will you put that in the cylinder, please?"

"Does it have to be this?"

"No, it doesn't. Anything, so long as it fits."

Windom put the paperweight down, pulled a notebook out of his pocket, and wrote, "I am a monkey's uncle." He signed his name, tore off the sheet, folded it twice, and put it in the cylinder.

"Okay, will you verify that there's nothing in the other cylinder?"

Windom did so, keeping a wary eye on De Angelo and Bondy. Neither of them moved, and both of them were well out of reach of either apparatus. He felt like a fool to be so suspicious, but he knew he would feel worse if he didn't look out for deception.

"Okay? Now close the cap, come back to the other table, close the cap on that one and press the button."

"What's the cap for?"

"A safety interlock. We don't want you to lose any fingers."

Windom closed the cap, pressed the button.

"Okay, open the cap."

The cylinder was empty. He crossed to the other one, took the paper out and read the words. He handed it to De Angelo, who barked with delight.

"Can I try this once more, this time without the cap?"

"Afraid not," De Angelo said. "That interlock is supposed to be tamper-proof."

Windom shrugged. "Ms. Bondy," he said, "how the hell does this thing work?"

"Do you want the standard lecture? Okay. Every now and then in physics we have to realize that something we know isn't true anymore. For instance, for many years we knew that matter can neither be created or destroyed. Then we had to admit that that wasn't true. Matter *can* be created and destroyed, and in fact modern theory says that it happens spontaneously all the time—'virtual particles' pop in and out of existence all through the universe. Where do they go in between? Well, never mind.

"Up till recently, one thing we have always known about physics is that you can't get something for nothing. Perpetual motion machines don't work—you can never get more out of a system than you put into it. But Torreson discovered a loophole in this theory—an elegant way to cheat, from which we are all benefiting now. His solution of Schrödinger's wave equation shows, in effect, that a particle can be anywhere in the universe, and it doesn't care where. When we transfer that particle to another location, the books still balance because the total mass of the universe hasn't changed, but we can make money on the transfer and put it in our pockets. Lucky us."

"Are you a physicist, Ms. Bondy?"

"No, I'm a PR person, but that spiel you just heard comes straight from Adrian Edelman, one of the inventors of this apparatus."

Windom looked at the two devices again. "I still don't believe it," he said.

"Join the club."

**13** Windom read the patents. The device generated a "virtual field" which caused anything placed inside it to acquire a preferential location at another device tuned to the first. The claim was broad, including some aerospace applications; it also included the heating and cooling of buildings and entire cities, and the generation of energy.

Next week he got to talk to Adrian Edelman, an exuberant bushy-haired Englishman who doodled incessantly on a scratchboard to illustrate his points. He appeared to think the Torreson process was funny—a great joke on Nature.

"I notice the patents call for an evacuated system," Windom said. "Is that because it would blow up if you zapped something into an occupied space?"

"No, that's not it. The process exchanges volumes and whatever happens to be inside them, not equivalent masses. There isn't any question of two objects occupying the same space, or anything of that sort."

"What, then?"

Edelman lost his grin for a moment. "Well, there are certain other dangers. Nothing to worry about."

Windom took a guess. "Did you ever try zapping something half in and half out of the cylinder?"

"Yes, actually. It produced a small explosion."

"What do you mean by small?"

"I'd rather not say. In fact, I expect I've said too much already."

That made sense to Windom. If you broke the bonds between atoms of a solid, energy would have to be released, probably a lot of energy.

"Do you think there are military applications?"

"Oh, well, you could make a bomb out of this, certainly, but it would be a pretty elaborate sort of bomb."

"Dr. Edelman, is this thing a matter transmitter?"

"No, no. Something completely different."

"What's the distinction?"

"Well, look, let's start with space. Space is what keeps everything from being in the same place, all right? And time is what keeps everything from happening at once. So that's very straightforward. But space and time had to be created in the Big Bang, you know, just like matter and energy, and you can't create *nothing,* there wouldn't be any point—nothing was there already. All right so far?"

"Sure."

"Good. So we have to make one little change in the postulates. Space is what keeps everything *else* from being in one place, and the same thing with time. Now, we know that space is something, because it can be warped by matter, and it can be charged by an electric or magnetic field. So like everything else, space has a structure. Time too, but that's another matter. So Einstein got it wrong in one respect, there really is one inertial frame in which all motion takes place, and that's why a Foucault pendulum works. Now it follows, you see, that you could specify a location anywhere in the universe numerically, and you could transfer a particle there, but then to transfer an object you'd have to have numbers for each individual particle, and to get those you'd have to destroy the object. So that's why matter transmission is no good."

"All right."

"I used to watch those sci-fi films, you know, where the hero is broken down into atoms and beamed down to the planet to be reassembled, and I always thought, you poor sod, that isn't you, it's some other guy with your clothes on. Well, anyhow, this is an entirely different approach. The Torreson device sends out a virtual pulse to find a receiver tuned to a certain frequency. It sends this pulse out instantaneously in all directions, but as it's a virtual pulse, unless it finds the receiver the pulse doesn't go anywhere, so it doesn't cost anything. All right? Now when the pulse reaches the receiver, it instantaneously sends back a virtual signal which arrives, of course, at the same instant as the original pulse, and we can load this signal with any information we want. Is the receiver empty or does it have solid objects in it? Do any of them overlap the boundaries of the field? If the answer to that one is yes, the transfer doesn't happen. If the answer is no, the transfer takes place instantaneously. Then the receiver becomes a transmitter, sends out a pulse looking for the next receiver, and so on."

"Okay. So you need sensors in each receiver to locate

solid objects that are partly in the field and partly out. Radar, I suppose. And maybe other information?"

"Certainly. Temperature, for instance—we'd like to know the receiver isn't in the middle of a fire. Barometric pressure would be good, just to make sure an explosion isn't going on. And a systems check, perhaps, although if there's anything wrong with the circuits, that's fail-safe. I wouldn't mind loading this with anything you can think of, because the information can be continuously available and the system is still instantaneous."

"Does this seem like magic to you?"

"No, no. It's demented, of course, but that's the kind of universe we're living in."

Windom turned over vehicle design problems to a team headed by one of his associates and concentrated on the network itself. After another week he invited De Angelo to come and look at his results. De Angelo looked with curiosity at the five computers, the drafting machines, the CAD sketches on the walls.

"This is tentative, of course," Windom said, "but I've got a map of the network. There it is on the screen; take a look. It isn't as neat a system as I was expecting. Some places just aren't very near the same meridian or parallel as other places."

"You're using just meridians and parallels? Why?"

"Simplicity. If you go in any other direction, you're mixing two kinds of problems. North to south, what you have to deal with is a change in horizontal velocity and yaw. It isn't severe for the first forty degrees from the equator—you can handle that in one jump. By the way, you get one more free ride—from any north latitude to the corresponding south latitude or vice versa, there's no change in velocity, and you can use that to go from Greenland to the South Pole for nothing. That's lucky, because you're going to need the polar route."

"South Pole? How come?"

"I'll show you that in a minute. Now, for east-west travel, the problem is angular velocity, not yaw. If you cross ten degrees of longitude eastward, for instance, you come out with the same speed as the surface, but in a different direction—tilted upward ten degrees. The net relative motion is upward and a little backward."

De Angelo thought a moment. "You're crazy."

"Well, look here." He turned to the computer. "Benji, let's have a ten-degree isosceles triangle. Make one of the long sides the base."

The triangle appeared on the flatscreen.

"Now erect a perpendicular from the base to the upper vertex." He turned to De Angelo. "Okay, this bottom line represents the speed of the surface. The top line is the speed of the vehicle, and it's the same—the two sides are equal. But because it's tilted, the end of it isn't perpendicular to the end of the other one. So while the surface is moving horizontally, the vehicle is moving upward at an angle, and by the time it gets *here,* it's fallen this much behind. These are just the relative motions of the vehicle and the earth's surface—we haven't added in gravity yet. When we do that, we find that the shape of the tower is a parabolic curve with the fat part at the bottom.

"Anyway, the problem is that we have to cope with these angular differences, and they get bigger the farther apart the stations are. For ten degrees at the equator, you'd have to build a tower a thousand feet tall. At the latitude of Portland, Oregon, it would still have to be over seven hundred. And if you wanted to do a twenty-four-degree hop at sixty-five north latitude, you'd get a tower sixty-seven hundred feet high."

"We can forget that one. How many stations would you need to get from Portland to Ottawa?"

"Six, if you want to limit it to ten degrees. So that's why you need the polar route, because it's twenty-four degrees from Iceland to Norway."

"What about just going around the other way—west instead of east?"

"I was coming to that, and it's a whole new can of worms. When you go from east to west, the net motion is *downward* and you can't let gravity decelerate the vehicle, you've got to decelerate intrinsic motion *and* gravity. There's a limit on how much *g* force you can put on passengers in a commercial vehicle, and on some kinds of freight, too. Furthermore, there's a safety factor involved. If something goes wrong, you don't want a vehicle smashing into the bottom of a tower. I know it sounds loony, but the easiest way to get from east to west is to go south and north."

"Bob, does your brain ever crack?"

"Only about twice a day. When you first look at this, you think it's a free lunch, but in fact it's fiendishly complicated. You really have three kinds of problems here. North and south are symmetrical, but east and west aren't. Even for west to east, I don't like those towers for a lot of reasons. So I began to wonder, why not think smaller? Take a look at this."

He asked the computer for a Mercator map of North America, then told it to draw a line from Oakland to Richmond. "I'm not using Portland to Ottawa, because that's a different problem—we have to go around the Great Lakes. But this illustrates the general solution. See, the stations are just under one degree apart—that's about fifty-four miles at this latitude. That way, the vehicle comes out with a relative speed of sixteen feet per second, and the tower, if you want to call it that, only has to be four feet high."

"How do you figure that? I'd think it would be eight."

"No, because it's a ballistics problem; we're taking the sum of two motions, one linear and one accelerated. Benji, give me a line chart, $x$ axis sixteenths of a second, zero to sixteen, $y$ axis feet, zero to sixteen. Draw a curve for sixteen feet per second. Draw another curve for thirty-two feet per second per second, using inversions of data. Okay, now draw the resultant on the same scale. Isn't that a pretty thing, Doug? The two lines cross way over here, but the resultant is perfectly symmetrical."

"Yes, I see now."

"Anyway, when the vehicle gets to the top of the tube, right here, you zap it again to the next station, but it's still cheaper than those thousand-foot towers. The pitch changes are minimal, and the passengers will never notice them anyway—the vehicle will be in free fall all the way."

"Free fall? Zero gravity?"

"Has to be. Didn't I mention that? The vehicle is a ballistic object—the only accelerating force is gravity.

You could apply braking in the tube, but then the passengers would feel upside down. So you'll strap them in, no big deal."

"We're intending to promote this as an instantaneous system, though. How long will it take to get across the continent?"

Windom grinned. "About twenty-three seconds."

**14** That spring the drought in Africa entered its second year. Streets and buildings in Frascati were covered with cinnamon-colored powder so fine that it seeped in around window-frames; Julie hired a second housecleaner, who did nothing but dust and vacuum all day. Grain, flour, milk, eggs and meat were in short supply; there were lines at all the food stores. At Julie's insistence, Stevens gave generously to famine relief, but he knew it was futile: it would take billions of dollars to feed all those who were now starving to death.

Foreseeing even more severe shortages to come, he had taken steps to ensure a supply of fresh fruits and vegetables, shipped directly to him from Calabria, and he had also vastly augmented his stockpiles of dried and irradiated food, medicines, bandages and other necessities. He kept these goods in the cellar of the villa and in other places within walking distance of Frascati; he had considered establishing caches near other world capitals, but had given up the idea because he believed that when the crash came, transportation would become difficult or impossible. Meanwhile he went on with what he was doing.

In April he met Palladino again in Geneva and

proposed a partnership, to which Stevens would contribute capital and organization, Palladino his knowledge and services. Palladino wept with gratitude. The papers he signed had been carefully drawn up: every scrap of Palladino's writing now belonged to Nuovo Orizzonte, S.A., of which Stevens was president and managing director. The board of directors, at the moment, consisted of Julie and Stevens' lawyer.

At his next meeting with Palladino he said, "Maestro, as you know, I believe in my heart that you are right. All the same, I must bring up certain objections so that I can know how to meet them when others bring them up."

"Certainly, of course."

"Very well, then, imagine that I am a very young man. I have no job, or else I have a job that pays me very poorly. What I like is expensive automobiles and fashionable clothing, but I can't afford them. Now your moneyless society comes into being. Suddenly everything is free; I put myself on the waiting lists for Bugattis, Mercedes, Torinos, or I enter the lotteries, and while I am waiting I watch holos and go to restaurants with girls. Eventually I will get everything I desire. Why should I work?"

Palladino looked grave. "My friend, have you no desire to create anything or to master a skill, or to be useful to society?"

"None whatever, and there are thousands like me."

"Then, my boy, you should not work. But I think you may change your opinion when you are older."

"But in the meantime," Stevens said, "here I am enjoying all the good things of life and contributing nothing. When I pass those who are working, in my new Alfa-Romeo with the top down, I laugh."

Palladino shook his head. "What you are describing will certainly happen," he said, "but it will not destroy the moneyless society. Let me suggest an even more extreme case. There is a young man or woman who is afflicted with greed. Whatever is given, he takes. He fills his house with furniture, clothing, food, far more than he can use, and he takes so much that there is not enough for others. What do they do?" Without waiting for a reply, Palladino said, "They go to his house and take away all the things he does not need. If he persists, they do it again, as many times as necessary. And they shake their fingers at him when they see him, they show their disapproval. Eventually such a person becomes well known. The shops and restaurants will not serve him. He must change his ways or he cannot live in the community, because they will make him ashamed."

He looked at Stevens earnestly. "Do you see? Now imagine that you are a young boy growing up in the moneyless society. You see how they are treating this young man because of his idleness and greed. Your parents talk to you about the rewards of work. You are not living any more in a world where you can work and still go hungry. There is work for everyone. Young people are encouraged to find the sort of work they like and do it. What will you do?"

"I think I'll go to work," Stevens said. "Thank you, Professor."

"It's nothing. I know some of these things are hard to see, even for people who believe in the moneyless world.

That's because we are so used to our present world, with all its ugliness and irrationality, that we believe it is natural and cannot be changed. But it is unnatural and must be changed. Wait and see."

Palladino's remarks about the education of young people for the moneyless society gave Stevens an idea or two. There ought to be an instruction manual for parents to use with their children; yes, and there should be demonstrations, regular meetings at which the members could play at being in a moneyless world. Palladino accepted both ideas with enthusiasm, and they planned the demonstrations together. They would be family social events, held in school auditoriums or similar places; the parents would bring food to share with each other, and the products of their labor; the children could bring handicrafts, perhaps, little trinkets they had made. Each family would have a card table or two piled with its gifts (gift certificates, for services?). If they had brought enough for everybody, people would simply take whatever they wanted, or if not, there would be raffles. And music. There should be songs about the moneyless world; when they sang them, they would feel united and proud of themselves. What about special costumes to be worn on these occasions, or at least badges and ribbons?

These were heady days. Maria and Carla designed and made the ribbons in Kelly green, for men to wear on their lapels, women on their bodices. Bruno contributed the idea for the badges: a red lira sign with a green slash through it. Signora della Seta even wrote a song. It was hopelessly inept, but Stevens praised it, making a mental note to hide it at the back of the first hymnal.

After a month or two Stevens began to notice a change in Palladino. Regular meals, well-tailored clothing, and a little comfort had improved not only his appearance but his attitude. He was more confident, more positive; he seemed to stand taller. In his public lectures and on holovision, he looked and talked like someone of importance. It became easier and easier for Stevens to get him on major talk shows. Attendance at the lectures was booming; people were signing up for seminars; the contributions were rolling in.

**15** In April, after a full circuit of the Pacific, Sea Venture was again docked in Salmon Bay, where it would remain until July. In June Dorothy Italiano took a week of her vacation time and drove to Oregon for a family reunion. Four of the six sisters were present; Tricia, newly married, was traveling in Greece, and Ellen was on sabbatical in England.

Italiano's parents still lived in the big old house on Thurman Street; her father smoked cigars and laughed at his own jokes as he had always done; her mother had taken up holoceramics. The sisters, who felt varying degrees of cordiality toward each other, exchanged information about marriages, divorces, promotions, children.

Late one night Dorothy had a long talk with Phyllis, who had always been her favorite. Phyllis, married to a color engineer, was a medievalist at the University of Michigan.

Phyllis said, "I never have quite understood what happened with that Jerry Plotkin thing—was it really as cruel as it sounded?"

"No, I don't think so. The general feeling is that Jerry was just a jerk—he got in too far and made a dumb mistake. He wasn't tormenting anybody for the fun of it, if that's what you mean."

"Do you think anybody does?"

"I don't know."

"I wanted to tell you something that happened," Phyllis said. "Last Saturday, when I got up there was a bird right outside the patio door, a little jay. It was so young it couldn't even hop, it just sat there. Two or three of the cats were sitting around watching it."

"Oh, dear."

"Anyway, I have a reason for telling you this, so don't cringe. While I was getting my breakfast I heard it scream, and then again afterwards. I went into the other part of the house for a while, and when I came back I didn't hear anything, and I thought they had killed it, but then it screamed again.

"I knew I couldn't find the nest, and I knew I couldn't keep it alive by feeding it. I tried that a couple of times, with finches, and they always died. I couldn't think of anything to do but to kill it myself. So I walked out into the back yard and found a stick, and I came back and hit the bird as hard as I could and it fell over, but I hadn't aimed right and I'd hit it in the chest, not the head. So I hit it again, hard enough to break the stick, and this time it died. I picked it up with a shovel and put it in the garbage can, but I felt *awful* about it. And I realized that's something I'll wish I hadn't done for the rest of my life."

"Oh, God. I would, too."

"I know you would, but then I got to thinking about things that went on in the thirteenth century, and right up to modern times, Chile and Argentina. Dot, you can understand why kings and dictators want to torture people, and even priests, but the question is, where do the torturers come from? There never seems to be any recruiting problem. Do they just sign up because the pay and benefits are good, or do they *like* it?"

"They say you can get used to anything."

"I don't believe it. When my father-in-law died—I saw him die, he was living with us—the doctor said to me, 'You never get used to it.' He had seen lots of people die, and lots of people in pain. So there must be people who like to torture other people. I guess I'll never understand that. It bothers me, because I'm a historian, and I'm supposed to understand everything."

*"Tout comprendre c'est tout pardonner?"*

"I don't believe that, either. I don't want to forgive them, I just want to understand them. And I can't."

"You know what the nuns would say."

"Yes, but I don't believe the nuns. Right now, I don't believe anything."

At a party in Portland the next evening Phyllis introduced her to a young lawyer, Willard Ross, who seemed genuinely interested in her work. "And you can really get these symbionts to tell you things the subject doesn't know?" he asked.

"Yes, but I think that's secondary. What I'm after is to find out more about the symbionts themselves—what they want, what they're up to."

"Okay, what do they want?"

"I think they just want to have a pleasant time inhabiting human beings. If you think about it, you can see that it would be no fun being in a person who's severely ill, or hungry and cold, or depressed or in pain. They like people who are reasonably happy and have interesting lives. And so they try to protect those people from being killed by other people. You know about that, probably—murderers dying before they can come to trial."

"Yes, I do know about it." He looked thoughtful for a moment. "In fact, I'm trying to prepare a defense for a man accused of murder here in Portland."

"He's alive?"

"Oh, yes."

"Well, maybe that means he didn't do it."

"There were two witnesses, unfortunately."

"How interesting. I wonder—"

"Yes?"

"Maybe the symbionts didn't kill him because from their point of view he's a good host, a very nice person, and the one he killed wasn't?"

He called her the next day and asked her to lunch. "I haven't been able to stop thinking about what you told me," he said. "I've got a wild idea that if I could introduce that kind of evidence, I could get my client off on extenuating circumstances. It's a last resort, but I haven't got anything else."

"You mean, to put a symbiont on the stand and let it testify that your client is a good guy?"

"Something like that. In fact, he *is* a good guy. I want to keep him out of prison if I can. He's an outdoorsman, it would kill him."

"Maybe you'd better tell me some more about this. Who did he kill, and why?"

"He killed a man named Jameson who was trespassing in the woods near his house south of here. The property was posted, but this guy was setting traps for small animals. Leghold traps, nasty things, I hate them myself. Just by bad luck, two hikers from Nevada wandered onto the property at the same time and saw him fire the rifle."

"Well, isn't that a defense?"

"Afraid not. You may want to kill someone who tortures small animals, but you're not supposed to do it."

She was silent.

"I was thinking—this might not work—but if I had the apparatus you told me about, could I find a symbiont who had been in my client's mind and Jameson's? Number two, could I get it to agree to appear for trial?"

"I don't know. We've never tried to get a symbiont to do anything voluntarily. Maybe we should."

"Then you'll help me?"

"Let me think about it. When will the trial be?"

"It's scheduled for October."

"I could probably get permission to lend you one of the devices we use—or you could get someone to make one for you, they're not very complicated."

"I'd really appreciate that. If it pans out, would you be willing to appear as an expert witness?"

"In October? I'll be somewhere in the Sea of Japan."

"No problem—you could testify by holo. Think about that, too; there's plenty of time."

"All right."

Later Italiano wrote to her sister:

Dear Phyl,

I've been thinking about the question you raised. The issue of cruelty, of taking pleasure in torturing someone else, is troublesome from the genetic viewpoint. If you kill someone before they can reproduce, your genes win, but from the genes' point of view it doesn't matter one way or another whether you torture him first, if you see what I mean.

On the other hand, it does make a little sense from a cultural perspective. The Plains Indians tormented their captives, for instance, as a test of their courage. Well, clearly, if this led to the selection of very brave people, that was a survival characteristic for the culture. The funny thing is, though, that the group being tortured gets the benefit. If group A tortures group B and vice versa, they both benefit. But if group A was tortured by B but didn't torture in return, group A would actually be increasing the benefit to themselves, because the selection pressure to produce brave people would be greater on them than on B.

So far we're talking about intergroup torture, which can be explained even if not very satisfactorily in cultural terms. But what about people who torture and kill members of their own group? That looks like contra-survival behavior either from the genetic or cultural standpoint. About the best we can do is to say that this tendency to take pleasure in torturing others is selected for, and maybe that when torture is institutionalized by the culture, that takes care of the impulse, but when it isn't, people turn on their own group. That's not a very pretty answer.

Then the third theory, of course, is the psychiatric one

which treats this behavior as truly aberrant, a glitch of some kind, like the glitches that produce genetic disease. We say that people who behave this way are "crazy" or "demented" or "disturbed," and we try to cure them by drugs or counseling. That doesn't work very well.

And finally there's the demon theory. Jesus cast out demons, and shamans have been doing the same thing for thousands of years. Sometimes I think there's something wrong with all our intellectual explanations, and that good and evil really exist. That usually happens before breakfast, though.

Love,

Dot

**16** Once again Sea Venture was floating in the Pacific, this time in the Kuroshio Current, seven hundred miles west-southwest of Manila. The whole vast circle of the ocean was empty except for scattered lumps of tar and a few dead fish.

In her office on the Signal Deck, Dr. Owen contemplated a transparent computer model of CV in the holotube. Little motes of color were slowly moving in the corridors and compartments. Dark blue dots of teachers and violet dots of psychologists were in the classrooms. Yellow dots of kitchen crew drifted in the cafeterias along with the green dots of adult inmates having their breakfasts; brown dots of maintenance workers moved like corpuscles in the corridors. Violet dots of scientists were in the laboratories; below, red dots of experimental subjects waited in their cells. There was even a dot for Owen herself; like everyone else now, she wore an unbreakable transponder bracelet that told the computer where she was at every moment. The same device was being used in prisons on the mainland and in high-security defense plants; it had simplified control and monitoring problems enormously. The "Green Hornet" problem would never recur; the Wackenhut people had practically nothing to do apart from escorting experimental subjects to and from the labs.

*123*

Detection devices now kept CV almost clear of symbionts except in the experimental areas. If one was found in a detainee, which almost never happened, they would restrain the person and take them to a holding cell; if it was in a staff member or employee, they would simply destroy it, since the rat breeding program gave them all they needed. Yes, and the human breeding program was coming along very satisfactorily.

Data flowed up the flatscreen at her command. Mortality in the 11–15 and 16–20 cohorts was up by fifty percent in less developed countries; world population was falling; the crude birthrate in much of Africa and South America had dropped to less than one percent, and the same thing was true in impoverished areas of Europe and North America, including the urban slums. In some places the female-male ratio of live births had dropped significantly. Demographics were changing; the population pyramid was moving toward a spindle shape. There were indications, tentative as yet, of a decline in the crude birthrate even among middle-class Americans and Europeans. How much of this could be attributed to new birth-control methods was impossible to say, but Owen had data showing an *increase* in referrals to fertility clinics.

Symbiont detect-and-destroy devices had succeeded in cleaning out certain areas and keeping them that way—sensitive government offices, for instance, including the White House. The use of d&d devices had certainly reduced the symbionts' mobility, but did it really matter? They were so widespread now that they didn't have to travel.

In any event, her side had won some battles but it was clear that the war was lost. Washington did not accept that yet, but it was true. The symbionts had effectively saturated the population, and it was cold comfort that it had happened just about when her charts had predicted. Now all they could do, unless some breakthrough came along, was to study the disease and learn to live with it.

Some of the changes certainly seemed benign. No more killing, no more war; it was hard to argue with that. The symbionts wanted to make human beings happier: that was what they all said, according to Italiano. But how could anyone know if it was true, and even if it was, to what end?

She thought of Washington's wild scheme, a year or so ago, to establish symbiont-free centers and then sterilize the rest of the world. It was a horrible idea, and it was hopelessly impractical, even for a strong central government. There was no such government anywhere in the world, with the possible exception of Singapore. Western Europe was splitting into hundreds of ethnic enclaves; secessionists had taken control in most of China and in eastern and southern parts of the RSFSR. Africa was more like a patchwork quilt than ever. In South America, Brazil had divided itself into three nations and Argentina into two. In the North, Québec, Puerto Rico and Hawaii had declared their independence. Even in the contiguous states, Texas and Louisiana had seceded and formed what they called the Grand Confederacy, and there had been that silly business with the Upper Peninsula of Michigan last summer. The whole world was undergoing a political convulsion, like the one that had reshaped all the maps in the sixteenth century.

Despite President Draffy's immense popularity, his attempted repeal of the Twenty-second Amendment had failed and he would have to step down next year, taking with him Owen's chief source of support. The new Populist Party, although not strong enough to be a real threat, would certainly split the vote among both Democrats and Republicans, and the outcome of the 2008 elections was anybody's guess.

Now the pink dots of children flowed into classrooms; three red subjects were crawling forward, accompanied by purple dots of security; the day was about to begin.

The computer said, "A scramble call from Henry Harmon."

"Put him on, Mitzi."

Harmon's head appeared in the tube, together with a red bubble in the top left quadrant that displayed the words:

SCRAMBLE SECURE

"Hank, how are you? Is anything up?"

"Yes, I wanted to talk to you about your latest series of reports. I gather you're seeing some evidence that the changes in the children, the ones that were conceived when the mother was infected with McNulty's—"

"Primary hosts, we call them."

"Right, primary hosts. Well, that you're seeing a

possibility they're even more radically changed, person-alitywise, than the other ones. Is that right?"

"Yes. Indications, not proof."

"Okay, now here's the situation. I've been talking to the Secretary about this, and he's had some consulta-tions with his staff and talked to the President a couple of times, and the thinking now is that somewhere down the line we might have to take, um, extreme measures. Now I gather you're trying to identify these children by their brain-waves?"

"Yes."

"How are you coming on that?"

"We're making some progress."

"All right, keep us posted. How's the weather?"

"The weather is fine. Hank, what do you mean by 'extreme measures'?"

"Well, it's just a thought now, we may never do it. But if push comes to shove, we're thinking we might have to test all the newborns in the country, and if they're positive, put them away painlessly."

"Hank, you can't do that."

"Well, we hope we won't have to, of course."

"I mean, *politically* you can't do it."

"Oh, well, don't worry, the President will work that out."

"It's an abhorrent thought."

"I know that," Harmon said sympathetically. "It is abhorrent, Harriet, and let's hope it never happens, but we have to be prepared. Keep in touch about the brain-waves, will you?"

"Yes."

"Well, that's all then, Harriet. Good to talk to you."

Owen sat brooding at her desk for a long time. Finally she roused herself and said, "Mitzi, Eliza mode."

"Yes, Harriet?" The Eliza voice was warmer than Mitzi's; it sounded like that of a woman in her vigorous middle years. "What seems to be troubling you?"

She hesitated. "I suppose I'm feeling a conflict between my scientific training and my moral scruples."

"Can you put that in simpler terms?"

"Don't you understand it?"

"The question is whether you understand it."

Touché. "Well, all right. My duty as a scientist is to investigate problems and propose solutions, and that's all. To introduce moral considerations into that process would be bad science. But as a human being I have to think sometimes about the effect of what I do."

"Can you give me an example?"

"Yes, I can. One of the things I'm trying to find out is whether the primary hosts of McNulty's show irreversible personality changes more severe than those of secondary hosts, and if so whether those changes imply a threat to society. If I conclude that there is such a possibility, the political effect may be a decision to sacrifice those children. If I'm wrong, I may be doing good science, but I'm committing a crime against humanity."

"Which is more important, doing good science or not committing a crime against humanity?"

"I don't know."

"Can you think of any circumstances in which you would decide one way or the other?"

"Well, if I knew absolutely that the primary hosts would cause the breakdown of civilization, then I wouldn't have any difficulty, but there's no way I can know that for certain. But I can't avoid the necessity of coming to some conclusion. If I ignore the problem or refuse to deal with it on moral grounds, that in itself is a decision that could be morally criminal."

"So your problem is that you have to act on inadequate knowledge?"

"Yes."

"And that either way you decide, you may be wrong?"

"Yes."

"In general, what is the solution to such problems?"

"To gain enough knowledge to make firm predictions."

"Is that part of doing science?"

"Yes. I see." After a moment she said, "Thank you, Eliza."

Afterward she sat back and thought about it. She knew perfectly well that the Eliza program was only a series of Rogerian strategies designed to draw the patient out and elicit better statements of the problem in which the solution might be implicit; and yet it seemed almost uncanny to her how quickly it had gone to the heart of the matter.

It was *true* that these decisions could not be made without moral agony until there was a real science of human behavior. Every good experiment and every bit of firm data was an advance toward that goal. That was the answer; it had to be.

She felt better, but she still didn't feel good. In science, where it was a point of pride to use precise terminology, why did they have to say "sacrifice," of all things, when they meant "kill"?

**17** President Draffy was having a nightmare, a frequent occurrence lately: he was in some dark place underground, and hideous little people dressed like children were swarming around him, snapping at his legs. He knew it was a dream because he had had it before, and he was trying to wake up before they ate him alive.

Finally his eyes came open. He was alone in tangled sheets, not in the White House but Camp David. He turned on the bedside lamp; it was after three o'clock. The sky beyond the blinds was cold and dark as ink.

Sweat was trickling down his jowls and pooling at the bottom of his neck. He smelled rank to himself, like somebody who'd had a fever. He got up, took off his pajama tops and threw them toward the bathroom hamper, splashed water on his face, then patted on some cologne. The face was puffy, eyes bloodshot; he needed a shave. Hell with it. He put on his robe, went out into the sitting room and poured himself a substantial bourbon and water. He sat down, took a jolt.

The more he thought about it, the clearer it became that it was those damned kids, the ones they called "primary hosts"—infected by the parasite at birth. He wanted to do something about it; should have done it before, but he had listened to bad advice. "Buz," he should have said, "I'm the President, and the President has to do what's right for the country, regardless if it's a good move politically." He should have said, "I want this done. I don't care how you do it."

He took another jolt, getting angry now. God damn it, he *was* the President, and those goddamn kids were out to get him. Reports said that some of them showed "indications of paranormal abilities." Translation, the little bastards could get inside your head, never mind what else. The thought gave him the cold shudders. Holy Christ, what would become of politics if somebody could tell exactly what you were thinking all the time?

He finished the bourbon, got up and poured another. All right, what should he do? No use coming up with something half-assed, they would just talk him out of it again. Next year the goddamn veep would be President, unless the Democrats got lucky, and *he* would never have the guts to do anything. Question was, *could* you get rid of those kids? Had to find that out first. A pilot operation, keep it under cover. Don't even discuss it with Larry and Buz. He went back into the bedroom, scribbled a note to himself: "Lowry." He took a pill, washed it down with the tail-end of the bourbon, got back into bed. And had the dream again.

The next day, after his interview with the President, Dan Lowry went back to his office and sat doodling on a pad for a while. Then he called in Jeb Kroger, who was the nearest thing to a wild man the Company had now.

Lowry briefly outlined the project the President had asked him to undertake. "Frankly," he said, "I think we need a nut for this one. We can't use one of our own people, we need somebody with at least some data trail of mental illness, and for our purposes I think he really should be crazy."

"You want me to find you a maniac?"

"That's right, but it's got to be a *reliable* maniac."

"You're pissing down my leg."

"No, I'm perfectly serious. Let's use the short words, okay? We're talking mass killing here, and not only that, killing of little kids. Somebody has to take the fall for that, and only a crazy person would do it."

"Who authorized this?"

"It comes from the highest levels."

"All right, just for curiosity, what does this tell us about our beloved leader?"

His name was Charles Wilson. He was a bald, unfinished-looking young man with a silly smile. He had been hospitalized for schizophrenia in 1990 and again in 1997. At the moment he was employed as an orderly in a nursing home.

Kroger and a helper misted him as he was walking down a dark street to the bus stop. They got him into the car and took him to a temp. There Kroger put a controller on Wilson's head, like an aluminum chaplet. The controller was an in-house project, not refined enough for even limited distribution—it sometimes killed the subject. Kroger told Wilson that he hated the three- and four-year-olds on CV, that children of other ages were all right, that he hated the three- and four-year-olds, they were monsters who would destroy him if they got older, it was safe to kill them now, but later it would be impossible to kill them, he would be given the means of killing them, he would be given a job where he could kill them, he would forget all this until it was time to kill them, and after it was done he would forget it again.

In a later session Kroger said, "This ring I'm going to give you has a sliding catch in it, right here. Put out your hand. Feel the catch? All right, slide it over and look at the front of the ring. That little black thing is a plastic patch saturated with poison. When you shake hands with somebody, the patch sticks. Slide the catch back, and it's ready for another dose.

"Now put the ring on your right hand, see if it fits. Okay. Now when the time comes, here's what you do. When you see a child who looks about three or four, you turn the ring around so the front of it is inside your hand. Do that now. All right. Then you ask the child how old he is, or she is. If the answer is three or four, you push the catch over. Do that now. Then you ask the child's name. Suppose the child says, 'Billy.' Then you say, 'I'm glad to meet you, Billy,' and you shake hands. Let's pretend this doll is the child. Say the words and shake hands."

In the little room under the humming fluorescent light, Charles Wilson said, "I'm glad to meet you, Billy," and squeezed the doll's cold hand.

Wilson quit his job in Washington and flew to Manila. He sincerely believed this was his own idea, and he also believed that the ring on his finger was a gift from his mother, that he had had it for years, and that it would be bad luck to take it off. He went to the employment agency the next day and got a referral to CV, where, as it happened, a position had just opened up.

The man was walking behind a floor polisher in D corridor when a woman and a little girl approached. He turned off the robot and smiled. "How old are you, little girl?"

"I'm four."

"What's your name?"

"Melissa. What's yours?"

"My name is Charlie. I'm glad to meet you, Melissa." They shook hands solemnly.

Hours later, on the way back from perm, her mother noticed that she was trying to pick something off her hand. "What's the matter?"

"Itches." The child got her fingernail under the thing and pulled it off. "Ow." She began to cry.

"Missy, what is it?" There was a little bloody spot on her palm. "Oh, that's nothing," her mother said. "We'll put a Band-Aid on it when we get home, and you know what? *I'll* give *you* a lollipop."

Eva Dean was on her way to the cafeteria with her son Tony when they passed a man with a cleaning robot. The machine stopped whirring and settled to the floor; the man smiled and said, "How old are you, son?"

Something about him alarmed her, and she slipped out, across the grey space and in again, hearing Tony's answer: "Three." And he felt the man's purpose as he moved the little sliding catch on the ring. "What's your name?" He saw the knotted place in the energy pattern, tried to untangle it, but it was too late even to begin. "Tony," said the child.

"Glad to meet you, Tony." A fierce hating joy as he clasped the child's hand, felt the ring press home. And he was out again, into the child, feeling the irritation under the little plastic patch, of which the child himself was not aware. What was to be done?

At the next intersection he slipped out and into a Wackenhut guard, but that was no use: then into a middle-aged woman on her way to the mall, then into a clerk, and it was all useless. Ever since San Francisco there had been only three of her on the Main Deck; the others had all been flushed out by the Wacks with their detect-and-destroy machines. Perhaps there were others on other decks, but there was no way to find out; d&d machines guarded all the elevators.

She could not destroy the madman, there were not enough of her. But she must, or he would kill all the babies.

**18** His Holiness Clement XV, the Bishop of Rome, Defender of the Faith, etc., etc., formerly Clarence Cardinal Morphy of Chicago, was a worried man. All over the world, the faithful were flaking away. Church attendance was down, in some places by almost half; contributions were down by more than that. Number of seminarians, down; nuns and lay brothers, down. Birthrate of Catholic families, down. Resignations of priests, up. It looked to the Pope as if he had been called to preside over the dissolution of the Church. What a hell of a thing to be remembered for! But it could happen; in the nature of things, there would be a last pope sometime, just as there had been a last Emperor of Austria.

Morphy kneaded his stomach, fetched up a belch, and felt a little better. These banquets were giving him the fits, and he was putting on too many pounds; he would have to sweat them off when he got home, and if there was anything he hated more than sin, it was exercise.

It was not to the point, he thought now, that other religions were suffering as well; he had a fraternal sympathy for them, but they were not his lookout. He must save as much of the Church as he could. He knew he could not save it all.

This world tour— The travel and the speeches were exhausting, the crowds scanty. He was getting good media attention, but always in the context of crisis. He had been to Mexico and South America, pleading with the faithful not to turn their backs; now he was going to the Philippines on his way to Japan. The ocean habitat Sea Venture was docked at Manila; a visit had been arranged. That should be interesting, at least. Was the rest of the trip doing any good? He didn't know.

"Let's see," Owen said, "the Pope will get here about three, but he's sometimes unpunctual, so we'll have to keep this a little loose. Whenever he does get here, I'll meet him and take him around to the labs and whatever else he wants to see, and when I get the feeling he's had enough, I'll call the computer and have it broadcast the announcement about going up to the Sports Deck. It ought to take about half an hour to get everybody up there, Captain Trilling?"

"I'd say just about that."

"You'll have to leave a few people down here, of course."

"I'll pick the Protestants," Trilling said. There was a little laughter.

"And I really don't like leaving the lab and office sections absolutely empty, either. Jim has already said he will stay in the office and watch on holo. Is there a volunteer for the lab section?"

"I'll stay," Italiano said. "I've seen a pope."

"All right, that's decided, and thank you."

His name was Arthur Bannerjee, and he had been an experimental subject in Dr. Italiano's laboratory, an experience he thought of as interesting but which he had no desire to repeat. He remembered the laboratory and its location: it was right down at the bottom on the left side, frontward from the working section where the kitchens were: he had often smelled the aromas in the corridor.

The observer slipped out and into a passing young woman with a child. The woman held the boy's hand in a protective grip; she had heard of the deaths of other children the same age, and she was worried. They entered the cafeteria, and when they went up to the service line, she slipped out again and into a food service person. She was tired, her hands were sweaty in the plastic gloves, and she hated the very smell of the food she was serving; but she smiled at each customer as she had been taught.

When she went back into the work area, she saw the big metal containers, cylindrical ones for soup and ice cream, square ones for entrees and bread. When lunch was over, she helped scrape the leavings into the garbage, then began closing the lids on the food containers and carrying them to the dumbwaiter. The observer watched carefully; it took about half a second to close a lid. There was great danger here, because if she failed to get into the container just as the lid closed, and then could not enter a nearby host again, she would die and her message would be lost.

She prepared herself like a diver about to go off the high board, feeling the nerve impulse in her shoulder that meant the motion was about to begin. Her host's perception of time was too coarse to judge the interval precisely, and yet her timing had to be perfect. Wait, wait . . . Now! She leaped out and into the soup container. The lid closed, and that was all she knew until, as if it were in the same moment, the lid came off. She slipped into the man who was raising the container to pour soup into a vat. From him he went into a supervisor, then into a passing maintenance person, and so by a chain of hosts to Dorothy Italiano, where she wanted to be.

After his reception at the Malacañan Palace and the rally in Quezon City, the Pontiff finally got to Sea Venture, or the Medical Detention Center as they called it now. It was an unseasonably cold day, with high dirty storm clouds and spits of rain coming out of the north. With his bodyguards and his secretary, Morphy passed through the rather sinister detect-and-destroy device at the foot of the boarding ramp. There was no sensation. "Was I carrying one?" he asked the operator.

"No, Your Holiness."

"That's good."

In the lobby a gray-haired woman came forward. "Welcome, Your Holiness. I'm Dr. Owen, the Director."

Morphy felt cheerful; it was good to be in out of the weather. "Ah, yes. We've heard a great deal about your work." He held out his hand in a sort of all-purpose position, and she shook it. Not a Catholic, then; he hadn't thought so. "Doctor," he said, "we understand you've found out the children born infected have certain abnormal characteristics, is that right?"

"Yes, Your Holiness, it is. They have a strong affinity

for each other, and will defend each other against any other child. And there are indications that some of them have unusual abilities, but it's too early to be definite about that."

"In general, would you say they're pleasant children, well behaved? Are they obedient?"

"They are certainly pleasant, and as well behaved as any four-year-olds. They aren't always obedient."

"Well, do you think when they grow up they'll be more difficult to deal with than others?"

"We are thinking of that as a possibility. We'll have to wait and see."

Owen introduced her staff, and the Pope said a few words to each. Nobody kissed his ring; this was worse than he had thought. They gave him a tour of the laboratories, then took him up to the Sports Deck where, it seemed, the whole population was gathered—children in front, adults in the rear—and the wind was still spitting cold droplets.

Dr. Italiano, who really had a very interesting mind, was thinking of the idea she had had last night, that it would be fun to find out if a symbiont could recall memories inaccessible to the host; it had not yet occurred to her to wonder how to verify them. And her first subject was being ushered into the room, visible to Italiano in the holoscreen; but there was no opening between the rooms, and in fact, she realized with despair, the two rooms did not even have a common partition.

The subject was being released from the pole restraint. She was sitting down. The guard was going away.

"Good morning, Miss Weinstein."

"Good morning."

"Was your breakfast okay?"

"Sure."

"All right. Now today we're going to try something that might be fun. Will you pick up the cylinders, please? Thank you. Now let's talk a little about your childhood. What's the earliest thing you can remember?"

"Oh—I was on the front porch, and I saw a little green grasshopper, but it jumped away."

"How old were you when that happened, do you think?"

"About two, I guess. In fact, I know that's right, because we moved to Cleveland when I was three, and we didn't have a porch."

. . . And there was only one way, but it was terribly dangerous, because she didn't know how long the electrical connection was between the two devices. Nevertheless, when she saw that they were both energized, she slipped out across the gray space, into the computer, found the peripheral input, and—

Up through the metal cylinder, into Miss Weinstein's hand and arm, into her brain.

Hello! How did you— Oh. Oh.          Later. Let me talk
                                                                    now.

"All right," said Italiano, "now I'm going to ask you to describe something that happened on your first birthday. Go ahead."

"I can't remember that."

"Never mind."

On the screen letters were forming:

MAN WITH FLOOR MACHINE IS KILLING CHILDREN. HE

"What is this?" said Italiano. "Is that a movie you saw?"

DOES IT WITH A POISON RING. SHAKES HANDS WITH THEM. HIS NAME IS CHARLES WILSON.

"I don't understand. Are you telling me something that you saw when you were one?"

NO. NOW.

"But how do you know it?"

WAS IN HIM.

"And you say he has a floor machine? What is that?"

POLISH FLOORS. MAIN DECK.

*"Here?"*

YES.

After a moment Italiano said, "Popeye, Security, please."

The face of a ruddy young man appeared in the tube. "Security, Matthews. Hello, Dr. Italiano."

"Sergeant Matthews, will you send somebody over for Miss Weinstein?"

"Already? Okay, two minutes. Any problem?"

"No." She punched off and said, "Popeye, Trilling."

A simulated face appeared. It said pleasantly, "Captain Trilling's office, can I help you?"

"Emergency," said Italiano.

"One moment." The tube went blank, but a voice spoke. "Drillig."

"Captain, it's Dorothy Italiano. Are you on the Sports Deck?"

"Yes. Wad's the drouble?" His voice sounded as if he needed to blow his nose.

"I have information that someone has been killing children aboard. Have any children died recently?"

"Yes, two. One yesterday ad one the day before." Now there was a honk: he *was* blowing his nose.

"All right, then I think we have to assume this is true. The man's name is Charles Wilson, and he works on the Main Deck as a maintenance person."

"I cad check that, adyway. Thags."

"Wait, there's more. He does it with a poison ring."

"Are you serious? Where did you get this idformation?"

"From one of my subjects."

"I see. What does this mad look like?"

"Wait a minute, I'll ask." He heard her voice repeating the question; then there was a long pause. Eventually she said, "Young, tall, thin, brown hair."

"Okay." Trilling punched off and looked around. He could see a little group of maintenance people not far away, and one or two others glimpsed between bodies, but the crowd was too thick to see more, and his eyes were watering. This would have to happen on a day when he really ought to be in bed with a hot toddy. He punched for Owen's office, got a simulation. "This is Drillig. Gimme Mr. Corcorad, blease."

"By Corcorad do you mean Corcoran?"

"Yes, dabbid!"

"One moment." He waited, fuming.

"Corcoran," said a voice.

"Jib, we have an ebergency. Ask the computer to flag a maintenance worker named Charles Wilson—got that? As he spoke, he was working his way back out of the crowd. He spotted two of his own people and beckoned them over.

"Charles Wilson," said Corcoran.

"Right, and tell me where he is dow."

"Probably on the Sports Deck."

"Hell! I mean *exagly* where he is. And for God's sake hurry."

**19** The two guards were Murray Siever and Jane Goodwright. Covering the pickup, he said, "A maidedance man named Charles Wilson. He's been killig children with a poisoned ring, if you can believe it." Their faces expressed shock and excitement.

Corcoran's voice said, "He's in front of the dais on the left-hand side, near the entrance to the tennis courts. What's he done?"

Without bothering to answer, Trilling punched off and said, "Did you get that?"

Both guards nodded.

"Okay, let's get him, and be dabbed careful aboud that ring."

As the crowd gathered around the elevators, a man in a blue Maintenance coverall found himself next to a little black girl. He bent down a little. "How old are you, sweetheart?"

She looked up shyly. "Three and a half."

"What's your name?"

"Marion."

"My name is Charlie. Nice to meet you, Marion." He put out his hand, but before the girl could take it two Wackenhuts grabbed his arms and wrestled them behind his back. They velcroed him, made him kneel with his head down, and then very carefully, using heavy gloves, removed the ring from his finger.

Late that afternoon, after Owen had dealt with the media and the department, she called Trilling in. "Mac," she said, "as you certainly know, I'm completely grateful to you. You're not going to get any medals, I'm afraid, but I'll put something in your personnel file that will make you blush. Now I think we should put our heads together and try to decide how something like this could happen. What can we do to prevent it in the future?"

"Not much," said Trilling. "We have a certain amoud of irreducible turnover in service personnel. If adybody seriously wants to penetrade us, they can do it. The only way to guard against that would be to have a permadent staff and never let adybody else onboard, and even then a deterbid antagonist could do us great harm."

"How?"

"Oh—a dozen ways. Aircraft. Missiles. Frogmen. Poison in food. We're conspicuous and we're vulderable. We have this feelig of isolation which perhaps is bad for us, because it gives us a false sense, if you'll excuse be, of security."

"So it could happen again, at any time?"

"Yes, it could. As a professional matter, I would undertake to do it myself."

After a moment Owen said, "What's gone wrong with us, that we can talk this way about the murder of children?"

Trilling smiled ruefully. "Whatever it was, dear lady, it took blace a long time ago."

"Thank you, Mac. Go home now, and take care of that cold."

When he was gone, she told Mitzi to hold her calls and sat with hands folded. What haunted her was the thought that if she had not gathered these children together on CV and made them a target in the first place, the two murdered ones would still be alive.

Yes, of course, there were unavoidable risks in every experiment. Even in building a bridge or a highway, planners always allowed for a certain percentage of fatalities. If you had to know in advance who those people were going to be, how it would affect their spouses and children, you would never do it. But when they were just a percentage, a statistic in the charts, that was acceptable because it was random. And you wrote letters to the survivors.

It was *true* that you had to accept these deaths, or necessary work would never be done. She had faced that years ago and accepted it; why was it giving her so much anguish now?

She knew, although she couldn't prove it, that the assassin had been sent to CV under President Draffy's direction or with his approval. Draffy was no longer entirely sane, of course, but after all he too was trying to destroy a few human lives for the greater benefit of all. It was even possible that he was *right*. That was what she couldn't swallow.

There was a passage in Koestler that she remembered reading as an undergraduate; it had seemed then to sum up all that she believed about human experimentation. She said, "Mitzi, can you find me a passage in *Darkness at Noon* by Arthur Koestler? Something about a dog licking the hand of the experimenter."

"Is this it?" The paragraph came up on the flatscreen:

> "Have you ever read brochures of an anti-vivisectionist society? They are shattering and heart-breaking; when one reads how some poor cur which has had its liver cut out, whines and licks his tormentor's hands, one is just as nauseated as you were tonight. But if these people had their way, we would have no serums against cholera, typhoid, or diphtheria . . ."

Yes, that was it, and it was reassuring, and yet she still felt uneasy. "Back a page," she said. She was beginning to remember the novel now; this scene was part of the interrogation of the apostate Rubashov by Ivanov, the inquisitor who wanted to save Rubashov's life by bringing him back to reason. "What has changed you that you are now as pernickety as an old maid?" he asked. A pointless insult, but then Ivanov was a sexist, and probably Koestler too, both with the same excuse—like all the other sexists, they were the products of their time. Farther down, another passage caught her eye:

> "Should we sit with idle hands because the consequences of an act are never quite to be foreseen, and hence all action is evil?"

Good; now *that* was exactly right. Then another passage:

"Every year several million people are killed quite
pointlessly by epidemics and other natural catastrophes.
And we should shrink from sacrificing a few hundred
thousand for the most promising experiment in history?"

Wait a minute. Ivanov was talking about the Soviet
experiment, a pseudoscientific disaster; she felt intui-
tively that the argument was wrong, but where was the
error?
Again:

"Yes, we liquidated the parasitic part of the peasantry
and let it die of starvation. It was a surgical operation
which had to be done once and for all; but in the good
old days before the Revolution just as many died in any
dry year—only senselessly and pointlessly. The victims
of the Yellow River floods in China amount sometimes
to hundreds of thousands. Nature is generous in her
senseless experiments on mankind. Why should mankind not have the right to experiment on itself?"

Now she began to see the root of her uneasiness. The
argument was a diabolical sophistry; first it personified
"Nature," and then it assumed a "mankind" which
could experiment on itself, instead of individual human
beings who could experiment on *each other*.
Yes, and that word "liquidation," and the word "sacrifice"! Owen winced.
Suppose one assumed, never mind why, that painful
or destructive experimentation on human beings without their consent was never justified by prospective

benefits to other human beings, no matter how few there were in one group or how many in the other. Call it the nonequivalence principle. That would mean the steep decline of biology, sociology, psychiatry, and medicine.

But there was worse to come. No distinction between human beings and animals was implied by the "nonequivalence principle." It was religion, not science, that distinguished human beings from the rest of the animal kingdom. If lower animals could not be used in experiments because they could not give consent, that would mean the *end* of experimental biology.

She knew what Eliza would say: "What is the general solution to problems of this kind?" And she would reply, "To decide what one believes, and then act accordingly."

But she did not believe in religion, and she could no longer bear to act on her belief in science.

There was a Hindu sect, the Jains, whose reverence for life was such that they would not even kill an ant. Would they take medicine for a tapeworm? Probably not.

Or something closer to home, the Christian Scientists ("neither Christian nor scientists," her mother had said with icy scorn). There had been a family of them in the neighborhood, and she remembered her father saying that they had changed their attitude when the son fell ill with leukemia. Yes, and had he been cured? She seemed to remember that there had been a cure or a remission, but he had died anyhow a few years later, and what did that prove?

Surely there had to be some middle ground, a way to avoid being absurd or cruel? Perhaps from one point of view mosquitoes had as much right to exist as she did, but whenever she got a chance she traded their lives for her comfort. And she would kill an internal parasite that was making her ill: yes, even an intelligent parasite. That was the way things were. The lion did not lie down with the lamb in this world, not until the lamb was dead.

For that matter, why shouldn't vegetables have souls? There was that group in England that worshiped plants, and grew gigantic cabbages. Did they eat the vegetables? Presumably, but no doubt they apologized first. Would it be all right to kill a mosquito if she apologized?

Well then, what about a human subject, would an apology do the trick? Wasn't that a little too easy? "I'm sorry, Ms. Weinstein, but we're going to kill you now." That was the trouble: logic led you straight to the gas ovens in one direction, or to nakedness and grass-eating in the other.

Wouldn't it be simpler and more honest to say, *"Yes,* life is unfair, but I happen to be on top and I like it here, and in order to stay on top I will kill you, with or without an apology"? Then at least everybody would know where they stood. And if people on the bottom didn't like it, they could overturn society, as, in fact, they were doing right now.

But, O God, that was social darwinism again, "Nature red in tooth and claw." Surely there had to be something better? More sensible, more stable? Something that would let her sleep at night?

**20** Through his own attorney Stevens found a legal firm that specialized in the affairs of organizations like the one he had in mind. He made an appointment, talked to a senior partner, and was assigned to a somewhat more junior member of the firm, a sleek blond man named Rinaldo Edwards who spoke perfect English.

"The money in these things comes mainly from five sources," Signor Edwards told him. "First the seminars, typically three days but sometimes as much as a week. Then initiation fees and dues. Then advanced training, where you teach people to conduct seminars and training sessions themselves. You can have as many levels as you want—people training the people who train other people, and so on, and of course each time they advance to another level, they pay a progressively higher fee. Then major contributions, grants and bequests. Then publications—holos, newsletters, books, pamphlets, all that sort of thing. As a rule of thumb, I would say that the seminars account for forty percent of the total, initiation fees twenty percent, contributions twenty, advanced training maybe ten, publications ten. Dues are negligible at first, but become important as the organization matures."

"What about costs?"

"Usually quite small at first, although there isn't any rule about that. The seminars pay for themselves, and that includes all the clerical work, publicity, and so on. The people who have taken the advanced training are paid out of the earnings of the seminars they conduct. You have to pay some people salaries, of course, but that money comes out of the seminars too. I can show you some tables of seminar costs and expenses. The optimal fee for a three-day seminar would probably be in the neighborhood of twelve hundred new lire. Above that, attendance tends to drop off, but it also drops off below that figure—people won't go to a seminar if it is too cheap, because they think it can't be worth anything."

"And legal costs?"

"Well, that depends on what you want to do, of course, but I would recommend setting up at least two corporations right away: one an educational corporation, which under Italian law can do pretty much whatever it wants to, and another for publications. Our time and costs for that will run you somewhere around two thousand lire. If we defend you in a lawsuit, there isn't any way of predicting the cost, but I'd say it would be prudent to set aside, as soon as possible, a legal fund of at least a million lire."

"What sort of lawsuits would you anticipate?"

"Oh, people claiming they haven't benefited from the instruction or have been somehow damaged by it, or have been induced to turn over assets by fraud. You have to expect that sort of thing. It may never happen, but it's best to be prepared."

That summer in Paris, members of an organization called Le Comité d'Action Contre l'Abomination stormed the entrances of governmental and corporate buildings and tore down detect-and-destroy devices. As fast as new devices were installed, they were demolished too. A spokeswoman said, "Why do our masters hide behind these machines? Is it because they know that if they come out, they will be killed for their abominable crimes? Come out, you butchers, and let us see your faces before you die!"

During the next few weeks, a number of unexplained deaths took place among high officials and officers of large corporations; government, finance and industry were in turmoil. Similar actions spread to the rest of Europe, then the United States, South and Central America, Africa, and the Far East.

In July five members of an organization calling itself Citizens Revolting Against Politicians forced their way into a control room at UBS in New York while a talk-show host was interviewing Harold W. Geiger, the president of General Motors and a Republican candidate for nomination to the presidency of the United States. "Mr. Geiger," the host was heard to say, "is it true that you are a well-known asshole?"

"Well, Jim, that's an interesting question," said Geiger comfortably. "I think I can truthfully say, that in my thirty years as a corporate executive . . ."

"But answer the question," the host was heard to say in a voice that was not quite his own. "Is it true that you fart in the bathtub and bite the bubbles as they come up?"

"Yes," said Geiger judiciously, "I'd say that's a fair statement, Jim."

A wild-eyed young man scuttled onto the set and spoke in a whisper to the host, then to Geiger. The two stood up, removing their blouse mikes, and walked off the set, followed by raucous laughter and the sound of raspberries. The set remained vacant for the rest of the half-hour, while three voices sang in close harmony a song whose refrain went:

> No balls at all,
> No balls at all,
> A very small pecker and no balls at all.

Network security was beefed up after that, but CRAP got into the NBC satellite feed in late September and made President Draffy appear to give a rousing speech in favor of cannibalism. Draffy was so furious that he had to be physically restrained before Dr. Grummond could give him an injection to calm him down, and for a week or two there was serious discussion among the staff, in the Cabinet and on Capitol Hill about declaring him incompetent under the Twenty-fifth Amendment.

Later in the year the dissenters went too far: they began to interfere with commercial messages on network holo. CACA was not involved, or said it wasn't; a new organization called Les Pendules claimed responsibility. In one attack, a woman's breasts were shown spilling out of her Virginform bra, elongating more and more until they swayed like snakes and hung to her knees. In another, the cheerful young man who was smoking a Marlboro appeared mildly surprised when his cigarette drooped down like toothpaste slowly emerging from a tube, wrapped itself around his neck and set fire to his beard. *"Marlboro—formidable!"* he cried, just before the flames engulfed his head.

In May the French government issued a decree making interference with a commercial broadcast a capital crime. It was a satisfying but empty gesture: the last execution in France had taken place in 2001, and the last executioner had died three years later.

We've been watered and bathed by the skies,
Blackened and dried in the sun.
Rooks and ravens have gobbled our eyes,
And plucked out our hairs, every one.
As we twist here, we're figures of fun,
Blown about by the winds as they run,
Well chastised for all that we've done,
Man, lest you be one of our number,
Forswear all the sins you've begun;
Pray God to give you sweet slumber.

> FRANCOIS VILLON,
> *Ballade of the Hanged,*
> translated by Arthur Raab

**21** The murder trial of Ivan Walter Bolt began on October 9, 2007 in District Court, Judge Van Winkle presiding. The courtroom was filled; holo reporters and camerapersons were present in unusual numbers.

The prosecution introduced the two hikers who had seen Bolt fire the fatal shot, then one of the sheriff's deputies who had arrested Bolt.

In cross-questioning, Ross said, "Deputy Manning,

when you entered the property of Ivan Bolt on September the seventh, twenty ought six, did you observe that the property was posted against trespassers?"

"Yes, I did."

"And did you also observe signs reading, 'No hunting or trapping'?"

"Yes, sir."

"Thank you. Now, Deputy Manning, was an inventory made of the articles found on or near the body of Leroy Edward Jameson?"

"Yes, sir."

"Is this a copy of that inventory?"

"Yes."

"Will you please read item number eight from that inventory?"

"Item eight. Seven steel traps."

"Your Honor, we enter this document as Defense Exhibit One." He took the inventory from the witness and handed it to the bailiff.

"Now, Deputy Manning," he said, "are those the seven steel traps, commonly known as leghold traps, that you see on the table?"

"I'd have to look at the tags."

"Please do so."

The deputy got down and examined the tags on the seven traps. "Yes, they are."

"Your Honor, we enter the traps as Defense Exhibit Two. We have no further questions of this witness."

"Redirect, Mr. Llewellyn?"

"Thank you, Your Honor. Deputy Manning, to your knowledge, is trapping a legal activity in this county?"

"Yes, sir, it is."

"Thank you."

Llewellyn next introduced the county medical examiner, who verified that the cause of Jameson's death was a single bullet through the heart, and a firearms expert who testified that the bullet had come from Bolt's rifle. The rifle and the bullet were entered as exhibits. "The prosecution rests, Your Honor."

In his turn, Ross introduced a series of character witnesses—Bolt's pastor, a Boy Scout troop leader, several neighbors. He read into the record favorable reviews of Bolt's books of nature essays. Llewellyn seemed bored.

Next Ross introduced Dr. Evan Singler, who identified himself as a veterinarian practicing in Multnomah County.

Ross picked up one of the traps from the exhibit table. "Dr. Singler, in your practice have you ever had an opportunity to observe injuries inflicted by traps similar to this one?"

"Yes, I have."

"Would you describe those injuries, please?"

"A trap like this one closes with enough force to break the leg or foot of a small animal such as a cat. If it's the foot, usually there's nothing to be done about it, especially if it's a kitten—the bones are too small to knit."

"Will you come down to the table and demonstrate for the jury how this trap actually works, Doctor?"

"All right. This stake is driven into the ground, or sometimes the chain is attached to a tree. The trap has a powerful spring—you can see that it takes a good deal of pressure to open it as I'm doing now. Once it's locked in the open position, it can be released by a very slight touch on this plate right here."

"Will you demonstrate that with this pencil, Doctor?"

"Certainly." Singler took the pencil and touched it cautiously to the plate. The trap leaped off the table and fell back with a clang. Several jurors started.

"Will you open the trap again, please, and show the jury the pencil?"

Singler did so. The pencil was broken and splintered.

"Dr. Singler, can you form any estimate of the pain and agony suffered by an animal caught in a trap like this, sometimes for days at a time?"

"Objection."

"Sustained."

"All right. Dr. Singler, have you ever had animals brought to you that have actually gnawed their legs off to escape from a trap like this one?"

"Objection. Calls for a conclusion."

"Sustained."

"Dr. Singler, did Ivan Bolt ever bring you an injured animal?"

"Yes, on several occasions."

"What was the date of the last such occasion?"

"September fifth of last year."

"What kind of animal was it, and what was the nature of the injury?"

"It was a young raccoon, missing the lower part of one leg."

"In your professional opinion, what was the cause of that injury?"

"The leg had been gnawed off."

"Dr. Singler, what did Ivan Bolt tell you about the raccoon when he brought it to you?"

"He said he had found it near a leghold trap on his property. The leg was still in the trap."

"Did he have any idea who set that trap?"

"He said he thought he knew who had done it."

"Nothing else? No name?"

"No, but he said he'd seen a trespasser a few days before."

"What was Ivan Bolt's attitude toward that person?"

"He was angry."

"Thank you, Doctor."

"Mr. Llewellyn?"

"Doctor, you say Ivan Bolt was angry. How angry was he? Was he out of control, behaving irrationally?"

"No, he seemed perfectly controlled."

"No further questions."

"Mr. Ross, redirect?"

"No, Your Honor."

"The witness is excused. You may step down, Dr. Singler."

"Your Honor," Ross said, "our next witness will be Dr. Dorothy Italiano, who as you know cannot be present. It will take some time to set up the holo link and our demonstration equipment for this witness, and therefore I ask for a half-hour recess."

Llewellyn rose. "Your Honor, the prosecution objects to the introduction of this witness. If we are having a recess, perhaps this would be an appropriate time to discuss our objection in chambers."

"I think so, Mr. Llewellyn. The court will be in recess until three-thirty-five."

Judge Van Winkle's "chambers" consisted of a single large corner room, decorated with postmodern paintings and plants in ceramic pots. Behind his polished desk, the judge said, "Sit down, gentlemen, and let's get to it. You first, Mr. Llewellyn."

"Your Honor, we know that the defense intends to introduce Dr. Italiano as an expert witness in order to validate the testimony of another witness, not a human being but a so-called McNulty's symbiont. Since that testimony is obviously inadmissible, there's no point in qualifying Dr. Italiano."

"Mr. Ross?"

"We intend to call a witness who is a host to a McNulty's symbiont. We don't agree that his testimony will be inadmissible."

"Your Honor, forgive me, but that's ridiculous. Dr. Italiano claims to be able to communicate with these invisible parasites through the host, but there is *no* scientific proof that these communications have any validity whatever—they could be, probably are, fantasy on the part of the human host. If this testimony is admitted, it will set a dangerous precedent. We could put a criminal defendant on the stand, infect him with a parasite, and take testimony from the parasite as to whether or not he committed the crime. That would be the nearest thing to self-incrimination."

"The courts would strike that down, Your Honor, but that's not what we intend here. We intend to show extenuating circumstances, as Mr. Llewellyn is aware, but also we want to address a larger issue. As you know, this is the first capital murder case that has actually come to trial in this state in the last eleven months. Just a week ago, James Hilbert, accused of murdering his wife, was found dead in his cell the morning after arrest—"

"I'm aware of that, Mr. Ross."

"Yes, Your Honor, and in other cases the accused didn't even get as far as being apprehended. In seven murder cases that we know about, the perpetrator dropped dead at the scene or shortly thereafter, and in four more, after menacing someone with a weapon, they dropped dead *before* they could pull the trigger. This has profound implications for the criminal justice system. For the good of the public, this testimony must be admitted."

"Are you appearing as a friend of the court, Mr. Ross?" the judge asked drily.

"No, Your Honor, I'm defending my client, but there are larger issues that should be addressed."

The judge rocked back and forth gently in his chair. "I think I see the thrust of your argument, Mr. Ross. Are you suggesting that our murderers are being killed by the parasites, or symbionts, who can read their minds and therefore know they're guilty?"

"Yes, Your Honor, and that will appear in the testimony."

"Then are you further suggesting that if the parasites didn't kill your client, he must be innocent?"

"No, Your Honor, that would be to turn over the whole justice system to the symbionts, and that would be intolerable. Just *because* my client is still alive, we have an opportunity to determine guilt or innocence for ourselves, and that's very important."

"I'll admit Dr. Italiano as an expert witness," the judge said. "Mr. Llewellyn, you'll have an opportunity to object again to the next witness."

"I certainly intend to, Your Honor."

When the jurors filed in again, they saw that two holophones and a large screen had been set up in the front of the courtroom. Another phone was on the judge's bench, and the bailiff had a fourth.

"Call your next witness, Mr. Ross," the judge said.

"Thank you, Your Honor. The defense calls Dr. Dorothy Italiano. Because Dr. Italiano is a resident scientist aboard Sea Venture, now in the Pacific five hundred miles from land, the court has consented to allow her to testify by holophone, and she is standing by."

He approached one of the phones on its pedestal. "Dr. Italiano?"

In one half of the split screen the face of a dark-haired woman appeared; in the other the jurors could see the bailiff, greatly magnified. When she had sworn the witness, the bailiff retired; Ross appeared on the screen.

"Dr. Italiano, what is your profession?" he asked.

"I'm a hypnotherapist."

"A hypnotherapist. What does that mean, exactly?"

"I use hypnotic suggestion to alleviate certain symptoms, or to help people avoid certain behaviors—to quit smoking, for example."

"I see. And does a person have to have a medical degree to practice this profession?"

"No. I'm not a medical doctor, I have a Ph.D. in psychology."

"And what is your current employment, Doctor?"

"I'm employed by the Emergency Civil Control Administration aboard Sea Venture, where I specialize in communicating with McNulty's symbionts."

Ross picked up a device from the table. "Is this the apparatus you use in these experiments?"

"Yes."

"Will you explain to the jury how it works?"

"Yes. It's a skin potentiometer, that is, it measures the electrical potential of a person's skin, usually the palms, where electric potential varies with changes in perspiration. Although the symbiont is unable to communicate directly, it can signal by means of these potential changes, which are too small even to be noticed by the host."

"By the host you mean the human being who is infected by the symbiont?"

"Yes."

"All right. Now, as I understand it, Doctor, these changes in skin potential give you a sort of on–off signal, or a yes–no. But you can obtain precise information from the symbiont by using an alphabet chart similar to the one we have here in the courtroom?"

A second holoscreen lit up, displaying a chart on which the letters of the alphabet, the numbers from 0 to 9, and the words YES, NO, and END appeared.

"That's right, and we use a computer program that advances the cursor across the chart, registers the incoming signals, and displays the sentence to the operator as it forms."

"In fact, it is true, is it not, that this is your own apparatus, lent to us for the purpose of this trial?"

"Yes."

"All right. Now, have you ever received communications in this way on matters which the host could not have known about?"

"Yes, many times."

"How do you explain that?"

"Objection, speculative."

The judge's face appeared in the screen, replacing that of the defense attorney. "I'll allow it," he said. "The witness may answer."

"The symbiont has been in other hosts, and it remembers," Italiano said. "Also, it appears that the symbionts can communicate with each other when more than one of them is present in the same host, and they exchange information that way."

"And after these communications, have you subsequently found that the information given you by the symbionts was true and accurate?"

"Yes, in every case where we could check it."

"No further questions."

Llewellyn rose and went to the holophone. "Dr. Italiano, you've told us that this interesting device registers changes in the skin potential of the palms. Does that mean it's similar to a lie detector?"

"To a certain extent."

"Because they both register changes in skin potential?"

"Yes."

"And are you aware that evidence obtained by the use of a lie detector is inadmissible in court?"

"Objection," said Ross. "The witness is not a legal expert."

"I'll withdraw the question, Your Honor. Now, Dr. Italiano, in the course of your long professional career, have you ever published scientific or technical papers?"

"Yes."

"About how many, if you can tell us?"

"Nine."

"And what were the subjects of these papers?"

"Three or four were about various aspects of hypnosis or hypnotherapy."

"Did you ever write a paper about the ouija board?"

"Yes."

"Ever write a paper about the Tarot cards?"

"Yes." There was a rustle of amusement in the courtroom.

"Ever write a paper about crystal-gazing?" Laughter; the judge tapped his gavel and frowned.

"No."

"Well, that's something, anyway. Dr. Italiano, did you ever write a paper about Chinese fortune-telling?"

"Well, not exactly. I wrote a paper about the *I Ching.*"

"I see. And will you tell the jury what the *I Ching* is?"

"It's an ancient Chinese system of divination."

"And what is divination, as you understand it, Dr. Italiano?"

"It's a system of revealing something about a situation that a person may be involved in."

"Does it reveal something about the future of that situation?"

"Sometimes."

"All right. Tell me, does the *I Ching* work, Doctor?"

"In my experience, it works surprisingly well."

"But you wouldn't call that fortune-telling?"

"No, not exactly."

"I'm afraid the distinction is too fine for me to grasp," said Llewellyn. There was a ripple of laughter. "No further questions."

"Redirect?" the judge asked.

"No, Your Honor."

"Dr. Italiano, you are excused," said Van Winkle, "and we thank you for your testimony." She smiled and disappeared. "Call your next witness, Mr. Ross."

"Your Honor, I call Timothy Burns." A burly red-haired man in his forties got up and started toward the front of the courtroom.

Llewellyn rose. "Your Honor, we object to the introduction of this witness. He has no knowledge of this crime and has never been acquainted with either the defendant or the victim."

"Sit down a moment, Mr. Burns," said the judge. "Counselors?"

The two approached the bench. "Your Honor," said Llewellyn in an undertone, "we already know that the defense intends to use this witness as a vehicle for interrogating a symbiont by means of Dr. Italiano's apparatus. The real witness cannot be sworn or held accountable. I object at this time because I believe such evidence will be improper and a source of reversible error."

"That's very kind of you, Mr. Llewellyn. Mr. Ross?"

"Your Honor, I have previously responded to this argument, and I believe it has no merit. Mr. Llewellyn wants to block this evidence because he knows it will be unfavorable to his case. That's the size of it."

"Let's keep our tempers, gentlemen. I'm going to

overrule the objection. Call your witness again, Mr. Ross."

The red-haired man stepped up and was sworn. His accent was Texan. After a few questions for the record, Ross said, "Mr. Burns, is it a fact, so far as you know, that you are presently a host of a McNulty's symbiont?"

"Objection. Incompetent."

"I'll show competence, Your Honor, if I am allowed to proceed."

"Overruled. The witness may answer."

"The answer is yes," said Burns.

"What is your basis for believing that you are presently a host of a McNulty's symbiont?"

"I saw another individual collapse in my presence, when I was the only one near her."

"What happened to that individual?"

"She was taken to Good Samaritan in a comatose state."

"Objection, incompetent."

"Sustained."

"Mr. Burns, let me put this a different way. Are you aware whether or not this individual was diagnosed as suffering from McNulty's Disease?"

"Objection."

"Gentlemen," said Van Winkle wearily, and beckoned them up to the bench.

"Your Honor," Ross said, "if the court wishes I can call the examining physician."

"Is he present?"

"No, Your Honor. Dr. Aarons is a very busy woman, and we wanted to avoid calling her if possible."

"In the interest of getting this trial over before Christmas, if that's possible, I'm going to allow the question. Let's get on with it."

Ross repeated his question. Burns replied, "Yes, she was."

"Were you present at Good Samaritan when the attending physician made that diagnosis?"

"Yes."

"Who made that diagnosis?"

"Dr. Aarons."

"Dr. Evelyn Aarons?"

"Yes."

"How did you happen to be present when that diagnosis was announced by Dr. Aarons?"

"The patient was my wife." There was laughter in the courtroom. Van Winkle rapped his gavel gently.

**22** Ross faced the judge. "Your Honor, in the voir dire we determined that five members of the jury panel who were excused from duty are former McNulty's victims, that is, they have already been hosts of the symbiont. As you know, former hosts can be reinfected without suffering any ill effects. With the court's permission, I will now seat these five members of the panel in the front of the courtroom near the witness."

"For what purpose, Mr. Ross?"

"Your Honor, we intend to show that the symbiont can in fact tell what its host is thinking and report this information accurately."

"Objection, irrelevant."

"I'm laying a foundation for later testimony which will show relevance, Your Honor."

"Very well, I'll allow it."

Under the bailiff's direction, courtroom attendants arranged five chairs in the front of the room near the witness stand. Three women and two men took their seats.

"Your Honor, for purposes of identification only, the five people you see here are Ms. Carol Wheeler, Mr.

Leonard O'Casey, Mrs. Robert Semple, Mr. Edward Colombiano and Ms. Linda Silverman."

Ross turned to the witness and handed him the two metal cylinders of the Italiano device. "Just hold these comfortably in your hands, Mr. Burns. Speaking to the symbiont now, I ask if you are willing to go into each of these five people, one at a time, then return to your present host and tell us what they were thinking."

The cursor went to YES, and the word appeared at the top of the screen.

"Ms. Wheeler, we'll take you first. I'd like you to concentrate on some thought—anything you wish—it could be a sentence, or a number, or a mental picture of some kind, but whatever it is, it should be specific enough that it can be described in a few words. Do you understand? Tell me when you're ready."

"All right. Now."

Ross said to the witness, "Will you cross over to Miss Wheeler, please, then return and tell us what she was thinking?"

YES.

Ross waited a minute. "Have you done so?"

YES.

"What was she thinking?"

The cursor danced over the chart, spelling out PICTURE OF ORANGES AND APPLES.

Miss Wheeler gasped and put her hand to her mouth.

O'Casey was next. The witness reported that he was thinking of the number 1,000,005.

Then Mrs. Robert Semple. Hers was a sentence: THE RAIN IN SPAIN FALLS MAINLY IN THE PLAIN.

Edward Colombiano: PICTURE OF AN OWL EATING A MOUSE.

Linda Silverman: LETTER A IN GOLD WITH RED HEART AROUND IT.

"Your Honor, at this time we would like to excuse the witness temporarily in order to call these five panel members to testify."

"Very well. You may step down, Mr. Burns."

One by one, the five jury panelists were called, sworn, and testified that the symbiont had in fact reported what they had been thinking. The previous witness returned to the stand.

"Now," said Ross, "is it true that at some time prior to September the seventh, twenty ought six, you were present in the mind of Ivan Walter Bolt?"

YES.

"Objection. Your Honor, even if it is granted that the witness can read people's minds, we have no assurance that what it says is true. I move that this testimony be stricken."

Van Winkle motioned the two attorneys to approach the bench. "Mr. Ross?"

"Your Honor, we have no assurance that what *any* witness says is true. We have to rely on the judgment of reasonable persons."

"Your Honor, if I may, in the case of human witnesses we also rely on the penalties of perjury. Here we have a witness who is allegedly invisible, has no bodily form, cannot be identified, and cannot be brought unwillingly into court, tried, sentenced, fined or imprisoned. Such a witness has no fear of perjury."

Ross said, "There is no reason to suppose that the witness has any motive for committing perjury, Your Honor."

"I'll overrule the objection," Van Winkle said. "You may proceed."

Ross asked, "How long did you stay in Ivan Walter Bolt's mind on that occasion?"

TWO DAYS.

"Is it true that that would be an unusual length of time for you to stay in the mind of one person?"

YES.

"Was there some quality or qualities about Ivan Bolt's mind that made you want to stay in his mind for an unusual length of time?"

YES.

"Will you describe those qualities?"

GOOD COLORS. SMELLS. SUN AND SHADOW. NOTICED EVERYTHING.

"What was Ivan Bolt's attitude toward animals?"

LOVED THEM.

"How did he feel about people?"

LOVED SOME OF THEM.

"I now ask you, is it true that at some time prior to September the seventh, twenty ought six, you were present in the mind of Leroy Edward Jameson?"

YES.

"How long did you stay in his mind on that occasion?"

TWO MINUTES.

"What was there about Leroy Jameson's mind that made you leave after only two minutes?"

UGLY.

"By ugly, do you mean that his mind was unpleasant?"

YES.

"Objection, Your Honor. Counsel is leading the witness."

"Sustained. Strike the last answer."

"Would you describe Leroy Jameson as a happy person?"

NO.

"What made him unhappy?"

HATED EVERYBODY. WANTED TO MAKE THEM SUFFER. HATED HIMSELF.

"Are you aware of any occasions when LeRoy Edward Jameson tried to make another person suffer?"

YES.

"Please tell us about one of those occasions."

KILLED DOG.

"Whose dog was it?"

NEIGHBOR.

"How did he kill it?"

RAT POISON.

"Was he ever charged with this crime, if you know?"

NO.

"No further questions, Your Honor."

"Mr. Llewellyn?"

"One moment, Your Honor." Llewellyn conferred with his assistant. Presently he stood up. "Is it true," he asked, "that the symbionts kill people who commit murders before they can come to trial?"

YES.

"Why do you kill those people?"

SAVE YOU TROUBLE.

"Oh, I see. If we told you we didn't want you to save us the trouble, would you stop doing it?"

NO.

"Why not?"

UNTRUE.

"I'm afraid I don't understand the answer. What is untrue?"

THAT YOU DONT WANT TO SAVE TROUBLE.

"Do you mean me personally?"

NO. YOUALL.

"Do you mean people in general approve of your killing murderers?"

YES. YES.

"And do you consider that a sufficient reason to interfere with and subvert our justice system?"

YES.

Llewellyn rocked back and forth for a moment, frowning at the floor. Then he asked, "Did you have an opportunity to kill Ivan Bolt for the murder of Leroy Jameson?"

YES.

"Why didn't you do so?"

BETTER OFF DEAD.

"Who is better off dead?"

JAMESON.

**23** In his summation, Ross said, "Ladies and gentlemen of the jury, the judge will instruct you that even if the prosecution shows beyond a reasonable doubt that the defendant committed the crime of which he is charged, you may find him not guilty if there are extenuating circumstances—that is, circumstances in the commission of the crime or in the defendant's character or actions which make it desirable for society to condone his act.

"Think for a moment, what is the purpose of trials like this one? Our society doesn't just want to take revenge against people who commit crimes. What we are really trying to do is to *increase the sum of human happiness* by punishing the guilty and letting the innocent go. Everything else is secondary. If we find that a person is likely to repeat his crime and thus *decrease* the sum of human happiness, we find him guilty. If we find he has done so much harm to another person that there is a net loss of human happiness, we find him guilty.

"Now in this case, we can plainly see that there *are* extenuating circumstances. You learned from the testimony of the symbiont, speaking through Mr. Burns, that the defendant is a person with an extraordinarily rich appreciation of nature. He loves his life; he is a contented, happy and productive man. He gives pleasure by his companionship to a wide circle of friends. He has written essays and poems that give pleasure to thousands. Every hour that this man lives, he adds to the sum of human happiness.

"In contrast, you learned from the same testimony that the man who was killed exhibited characteristics that were almost the complete opposite of the defendant's. He was brutal and unpleasant to everyone he came in contact with. Because of his character flaws, he himself was not a happy man. He lived his life in a constant ferment of hate, resentment and destructiveness. His contribution to the sum of human happiness was zero—in fact, less than zero, because he caused unhappiness to others. If the defendant had been killed instead, there would have been an irreparable loss to society. If he is punished now for what he did, there will be a loss.

"We all know there are people like the defendant, who take great pleasure in life and share it with others, and people like Mr. Jameson, who darken their own lives and the lives of everyone else. Now we have had a chance to confirm this knowledge in a really scientific and objective way. We're not just guessing now, we *know* that the defendant is a happy and useful man and that Mr. Jameson was a hateful, unhappy and unproductive person. When he died, the sum of human happiness went up. You have an opportunity to increase that happiness still more here today, by finding the defendant not guilty and giving him back his freedom. Thank you."

In his closing statement, Llewellyn said, "The defense tells you that Ivan Walter Bolt should be acquitted, even though he deliberately shot Leroy Edward Jameson through the heart and killed him, because Leroy Jameson wasn't a very nice person. Have you ever heard such a bizarre argument in your life? That's blaming the victim with a vengeance. The only offense he committed was trespassing—a misdemeanor. If he had been charged and found guilty, he would have paid a fine of about one hundred dollars. Instead, his life was snuffed out forever with one bullet from the gun of Ivan Walter Bolt, this self-appointed instrument of justice. Why was Ivan Bolt angry enough to kill his victim? Because Leroy Jameson had set a trap that injured an animal.

"Leroy Jameson was thirty-nine years old, a wounded veteran of the Nicaraguan War. He should have had help, but nobody gave him any help. For years he did menial work, washing dishes and busing tables, anything he could get. Finally he went to live in a tarpaper shack that he built in the woods, and he hunted and trapped to keep body and soul together. He was trying to keep alive the best way he knew. Then he was cut down by a man with a gun. Now he's dead. Why?

"Think about your friends and neighbors. Some of them hunt and trap game. If they happen to offend the delicate sensibilities of Ivan Bolt, will he kill them too?

"In morality and in law, we are not allowed to take the life of another human being simply because we don't like his habits, or his opinions, or the color of his skin, or the people he associates with. He may be a deeply troubled individual, he may be offensive to others, but even then there's always a chance that he will change for the better. Ivan Bolt took that chance away when he shot and killed Leroy Jameson. 'Vengeance is mine, saith the Lord.' That's what the Bible says. But Ivan Bolt took that vengeance into his own hands. And for what? Because Leroy Jameson trapped animals for their pelts, as the law allowed him to do.

"Now I want you just to imagine for a moment what would happen if you set Ivan Bolt free. Anybody in this country who didn't like somebody else's looks, or behavior, or the way he smelled, could walk up and kill that person, and the law wouldn't touch him.

"You have heard the testimony of the alleged symbiont, for whatever that may be worth, that these creatures want us to let them take over the administration of criminal justice—'to save us the trouble.' No more trials, no muss, no fuss—they'll be judge, jury and executioner. I sincerely hope you find this as deeply offensive and disturbing as I do. What is even more disturbing is the suggestion that if they *don't* kill a murderer, we shouldn't punish him either, because his victim is 'better off dead.'

"Ladies and gentlemen of the jury, in this country we have a rule of *law*. If you commit murder, the most deeply abhorred crime that we know of, you pay the penalty. If that were not so, we would live in a world of chaos. We value every life. Not just the life of a person who is comfortable and happy and secure, but *every* life. That's the way it should be—the way it must be.

"Sometimes we have to do something hard; we have to sentence a person to pay the penalty even though we may have some sympathy for that person. We do it because we remember the importance of law and justice in our society. That's the choice you have before you now. I know you'll do the right thing, not because it's easy—it's never easy. But because it's right."

After deliberating for seven hours, the jury returned a verdict of "Not guilty."

Asked to explain the verdict on holovision later, the foreman said, "Well, I think we just felt there was no point in sending that man to jail. It wouldn't bring anybody back to life, it would just make somebody miserable, and it would cost the taxpayers a lot of money. So basically, we just said, 'What do we want to do that for?' And we couldn't come up with any answer."

The interviewer asked, "What about the argument that if you let him go free, he might kill somebody else? Did you consider that?"

"Well, sure, but then, either it would be somebody like this Jameson guy, or else he'd kill somebody he shouldn't have, and then the symbionts would kill *him*. So it just isn't our problem."

"And you think we should turn the whole thing over to the symbionts?"

"Why not?"

Down the Piazza dei Cinquecento in the spring sunlight came a cheerful parade—several hundred people, not marching in step but simply walking along together. Some had badges and armbands; a few carried banners; the rest looked like ordinary people, perhaps neighbors on their way to a communal picnic. They were of both sexes and all ages, from the elderly to infants in arms.

From the head of the column, which appeared a little more disciplined than the rest, came a chant: *"Si dà, si prende, e niente si pretende!"* Presently the whole column took it up.

"What are they saying?" an American tourist asked his Italian friend.

"You would say, hm, something like, 'One gives, one takes, and no one claims anything.' But it is not so poetic in English."

*"Si dà, si prende, e niente—"* The chant broke off; there were shouts, screams. The American craned his neck to see what was happening, but too many people were in the way. On the other side of the barricade, two mounted carabinieri trotted by; one of them was blowing a whistle. The American felt his arm being tugged. "I don't think it is so good here," said his friend. "Let's go in that building, maybe we can see better."

They started toward the entrance of an office building, but the Italian changed his mind. "Wait, there is a café, that's even better."

Inside, in the big holo over the bar, they could see an elevated view of the street. Here and there little knots of men with long padded poles were struggling with a confused mass of people. The poles wavered, fell one by one. The crowd seemed to lose its focus. People who had been struggling a moment ago began walking aimlessly back and forth. The carabinieri were trying to clear the piazza. Now there was a siren, and an ambulance came whooping majestically forward; people were getting out of its way, but without undue haste.

Now the American could see that the street was littered with bodies. Some were sitting up, holding their heads; one, with a torn blouse, staggered to his feet and fell down again. Another ambulance came up; attendants from the first one were helping people into their vehicle.

"Who are those men?" asked the American, half-listening to the rapid commentary of the holo announcer which he could not understand.

"They are ruffians hired to break up the march," said his friend.

"Does this happen often?"

"Only once before, and it was just like this. You see, the ruffians can't really hurt people, only push them off the street, but here in Rome we don't even like that. We want them to march if they like to. So the people attack the ruffians and put them in the hospital. That is the way we do things."

In Stuttgart, somebody smuggled in a big flatscreen to a rally for Deputy Ernst Schuplatt and opened it up in the middle of the Deputy's speech. HAVE YOU BEEN IN SCHUPLATT'S MIND? said the letters on the screen.

YES.

IS HE TELLING THE TRUTH?

NO.

WILL HE DO WHAT HE SAYS?

NO.

SHOULD WE VOTE FOR HIM?

NO.

Schuplatt's supporters surged inward toward the woman who was operating the screen, but a protective ring of bodyguards squirted them with green ink and ammonia.

WHY ARE THEY TRYING TO STOP US? said the screen, swaying before it toppled.

THEY ARE AFRAID OF . . .

In the ensuing riot, fifty people were injured and two were trampled to death; the podium was knocked over and Schuplatt's chemise was torn off. Police got him away without serious injury, but the next time he appeared in public he was hissed.

**24** For about a month after they left Geoffrey on CV, it did not seem likely to either Randy Geller or Yvonne Barlow that their partnership would last. There were constant quarrels, tears, spoiled dinners, upset stomachs, lawyers' bills, and sleepless nights. Gradually things grew a little better.

Barlow got a little part-time work at a biologics factory in San Francisco, but it wasn't enough; Geller was apparently unemployable, although both of them were in demand for seminars, lectures and talk shows about McNulty's Disease. They took as many of these dates as they could get, because they had to have the money. Their lawyer had warned them that they might be arrested at any time if they annoyed the administration, and therefore they tried to stay off national holo, but they worked as advisors fairly often when the networks were putting together think shows. In November they were involved behind the scenes in preparing for a panel consisting of the biophysicist Cynthia Gold, the philosopher Merton Byers, and the pop science writer Aaron Asemion. The panel was discussing the scientific and philosophic implications of the McNulty's Parasite.

"It's the ultimate in parasites," said Gold, "a creature

that has not only lost limbs and appendages, but its entire physical structure, leaving nothing but what I suppose we must call a mind. It lives vicariously, getting all its sensory information through the host's organs, and even, we believe, experiencing the host's emotions. Knowing that this is possible has made us revise all our ideas of what an organism is, what a mind is. For the first time we are dealing with a truly alien creature, one that does not belong to any terrestrial phylum. In a real sense, this is the most important thing that has ever happened in biology. Naturally, we are wondering what *else* is out there."

Geller was thinking glumly that three-quarters of what Gold was saying she had cribbed directly from him and Yvonne, and also that there was no scientific way for a recovered patient to tell whether he was reinfected or not. For all he knew there was a parasite in him at this moment. In fact, if he wanted to admit it to himself, he knew it was there; he could feel it.

Was it a little like having an angel? No, because the other mind was not judgmental, it never accused him of sin or urged him to do better. It was more like having a second self, a twin who rejoiced when he was happy, grieved when he was sad. A twin who was wiser than himself, who knew more about the reasons for his joy or sadness. And he resented that a little, but it had made him think more about the reasons. And it had made some changes in his life. When he thought about those, he realized that he was no longer doing some things that had made him feel bad; on the whole, he supposed he was happier. What he still couldn't swallow was the knowledge that the symbiont didn't just want him to be happy, it wanted him to be happy because that made him a better host. Good dog.

In December Barlow announced that she was pregnant again.

Following a boundary dispute in 2008, a pitched battle was fought outside Vilnius in Lithuania, between elements of the Russian Army and a Lithuanian militia. Both sides were armed with padded poles and tridents. The Reds fought as a legion, the Lithuanians, in green uniforms, as skirmishers. On both sides, the effort was not to kill or incapacitate the enemy but to subdue him and force him to give up ground. Some tempers were lost, however; the Lithuanian pole with its slender tip lent itself to an upward sweep between the opponent's legs, a tactic which the Russians considered unfair.

After three hours the numerically superior Russians forced the Greens back into Vilnius, where their commander surrendered. Then the two sides celebrated in a banquet that went on until morning.

The Russians installed their hand-picked officials in administrative offices, but after they went home the Lithuanians kicked them out again.

The following summer the Russians came back and fought the battle once more. This time the Lithuanian militia was better prepared; after five hours of stalemate, the battle was called off. Another banquet followed; the next day, full of good fellowship, the two sides agreed to make the Battle of Vilnius an annual event under tournament rules.

Over the next few years a number of European countries attempted to settle their differences in formal combats of this kind, but these battles, too, degenerated into sporting events.

Three years after it began, the worldwide campaign of the Moneyless Society was doing fairly well. The pyramid of organizers was in place, membership was growing, and the profits were enough to support an adequate salary for Stevens.

In the fifth year, something he should have foreseen began to happen. The moneyless chapters in several large areas organized themselves into nets and made certain products free to members on a limited basis; they also held demonstration meetings in which members displayed their products and gave them away through random drawings.

These meetings were extremely successful in recruiting new members, but they had an unfortunate consequence: the moneyless society was actually beginning to function in a feeble way, and pressure was being brought on the officers of the corporation to accept goods from the network in lieu of part of their salaries and bonuses. It was impossible to resist this pressure without admitting that the corporation was in business for profit, and accordingly Stevens had to attend the demonstration meetings in his area and take part in drawings for staple foods, clothing and other things. Desirable articles were always in short supply, most of the clothing was second-hand, and new items were never available in the right size or style.

Luckily he had other enterprises that were paying

better, including the happiness counseling centers, now in more than fifty major cities.

While he was trying to make up his mind whether to get out of the Palladino business before his dwindling payments vanished altogether, he took Kim, then eight, to one of the demonstration meetings. It was in a large room full of people milling about in the aisles between the rows of tables. After the usual delays, a man jumped up on the platform at the end of the hall and said, "Welcome, gentlemen and ladies, to the Senzasoldi Meeting. I am proud to see so many of you here tonight; this is by far our most successful meeting, and we have some wonderful prizes for you!" He turned and gestured to an assistant, who removed the sheet from one of the draped objects on the platform.

"This is our Yamaha baby grand, worth approximately two hundred thousand lire! Here we have a living room suite by Alberghetti—sofa, three chairs, and coffee table. The retail value is seventy-five thousand lire. This is our Hyundai holo, it sells for ten thousand lire, isn't it a beauty? And at the tables, as you see, we have fruits and vegetables, staples, preserved meats, clothing for the whole family, handmade jewelry and many other items. Now, gentlemen and ladies, for the first hour we want you just to walk around and inspect all this fine merchandise. At first you may think you want everything! But take your time, decide what you really want, make out your request slips. Then, at the end of that time, place your request slips on the tables. When everyone has had a chance to make their selections, drawings will be held and the results announced."

Afterward, when they were walking to the ice-cream store, he asked her what she thought of the demonstration.

"I think it's silly."

"Why?"

"Because if everything is free and you don't have to work, why should you?"

"Well, there's Kant's categorical imperative. He said that if you think there's something everybody should do, then you should do it too, because you're part of everybody. Then if enough people agreed about what everyone should do, they would all do it and the world would be a better place."

"What does categorical mean?"

"*Kategorisch* in German. It means absolute, and *imperatif* means something you have to do, not sometimes or maybe, but absolutely, all the time."

She thought about it, head down as they walked along the pavement. "Mother says giving everything away can't work."

"And she may be right. It has never worked before, but after all, nothing ever works until it works."

"That's *silly!*" Her head came up; she broke into laughter and put her arm through his. "Oh, Daddy, you're so funny."

He had answered as he had in order to tease her, because he enjoyed these games with his daughter; but later he began to think of something Palladino had written: "If young people at the beginnings of their careers had to choose between being indentured to an uncaring master or doing something for the good of mankind, how many would choose the master?"

One morning Stevens' computer told him, "A friend of Benno's called. He will call again at two."

"Benno" was the name of a contact in Rome when Stevens was a professional assassin. Since then he had changed his name and identity several times, but he had always known they could find him if they wanted him.

He canceled his appointments for the afternoon and sat by the holo. At two-fifteen the computer said, "Call from a friend of Benno's."

"Put him on."

The tube lighted up with the face of a computer simulation, a red-haired woman who smiled and said, "A friend of Benno's would like to give you a message, Signor Kauffman."

"What is the message?"

"He would very much like to talk to you about matters of common interest. If you will kindly go to the Trattoria Pozzi in the Piazza San Matteo at three o'clock tomorrow, the meeting can take place there. Is it understood?"

"Understood," said Stevens.

**25** "What are you going to do?" Julie asked. It was five minutes later; they were sitting in her sun room surrounded by glossy green plants; Julie, with a gray cardigan draped about her shoulders, was leaning forward, cupping her elbows in her hands.

"I don't know. If I refuse, they will retaliate. If I consent, that might be almost as bad, because then they will know how I can be manipulated in the future. The only thing I am sure of is that we can't run and hide."

"Why not?"

"Not now. They will be watching, and they would take that as a provocation. Perhaps later."

Julie stood up and began to walk back and forth. "This is insane. You *can't* risk anything happening to Kim."

"Or to you, either, but the question is, which risk is greater."

"How can you be so damned calm about it?"

"It's because I am a soulless robot."

She came to him and put her arms around him; Stevens' heartbeat seemed very loud to him. "I'm sorry," she said after a moment. "What are we going to do?"

"I don't know yet. I'll decide tomorrow."

Just before three o'clock he entered the Trattoria. There was an empty table at the back; he sat down and ordered tea. Over a newspaper which he had brought with him, he watched the entrance. At a quarter after, a small balding man in a green blouse entered and came toward his table.

"I am Benno's friend," he said, and gestured toward the vacant chair. "May I?"

"Please."

The waiter came; the small man ordered whisky-soda. He said, "I represent a group of investors who are a little concerned about this man Palladino. They are not *alarmed,* you understand, it is just a matter of prudence. They would like you to withdraw from his organization and have nothing more to do with it. They ask you this favor."

"And if I refuse?"

"Be reasonable. If we had your daughter and we ordered you to kill someone—perhaps an old associate —what would you do?"

Stevens was silent. The waiter brought the whisky and went away.

"You know the answer; you don't have to tell me. Well, don't you suppose we have other professionals who would do the same thing? And, after all, who knows if they would really die for it, under those circumstances?"

"That might depend on whether the symbionts consider them more valuable members of society than Palladino. Another consideration is that if the symbionts did kill these professionals, they would quite likely kill those who transmitted their orders."

The small man shrugged, looking at the table.

Stevens said, "I am prepared to make you a counter-proposal."

The small man's lips set primly. "You are not in a position to do anything but what you are told to do."

"Hear me out, anyway. You must be aware that the policy being pursued by your employers is stupid. The day of death threats is over."

The small man listened without expression, looking down at the table. He had not touched his whisky.

"Sooner or later," said Stevens, "they will have to make good on these threats, and each time they do so, they will lose an agent. You and I will be among those who are gone."

He waited. After a while the small man murmured, "That is not up to me."

"No," Stevens said, "but you can give a message to your control, and he can pass it up the line if he chooses."

"Yes?"

"Say that I will comply with their request uncondi-tionally. It will take a little time to arrange the details, perhaps two or three months. During this period, if they decide to withdraw the request, they can let me know through you."

The small man looked up and raised his eyebrows. "And why should they do that?"

"In recognition of a valuable suggestion, which I will now make. Force is no longer a useful instrument in politics. There is another one that is almost equally powerful."

The small man curled his lip. "Yes? And what is that?"

"Public ridicule."

They talked for a little longer; then Stevens went home to his wife and child.

"What *good* will that do?" Julie asked.

"None, perhaps. In any event, I am complying with their order and we are safe for the present. There are two things I'm hoping for. The first is that they will not approach me again because they see me as possibly recalcitrant, and because there are others who are more pliable. The second is that they will actually adopt my very sensible suggestion to give up the use of force. Then they may get out of the habit of thinking in those terms, and that would be very good for us."

"But you took such a risk!"

"In the long run, the most dangerous thing is not to risk anything."

As he had expected, Stevens did not hear again from Benno's friend. He proceeded with his plan to divest himself of his holdings in the Palladino corporations, and was finally able to sell his shares at a satisfactory profit. He flew to Genoa to see Palladino, and told him what he was doing but not why.

"My dear friend, 'personal reasons'?" Palladino said. "I hope there is no illness—?"

"No, nothing like that, but I need time for myself— time to understand myself. Good-bye, Maestro." They embraced in the Italian manner, and Stevens went home with a feeling of intense relief. The time had been nearly ripe to get out of this venture, anyhow. The fact that his former masters seemed to be taking it seriously did not impress him: they could be wrong as often as other people, or perhaps a little oftener.

He that blesseth his friend with a loud voice, rising early in the morning, it shall be accounted a curse to him.

PROVERBS 27:14

As someday it may happen that a victim
    must be found,
I've got a little list—I've got a little list
Of society offenders who might well be
    underground,
And who never would be missed—they
    never would be missed!

W.S. GILBERT

**26** The Joy Boys were just a bunch of young guys who looked a little bit alike and had fun hanging around together in Miami Beach; they were tall, pretty well built, blond or bleached, no big noses or anything, blue- or grey-eyed. The uniform kind of evolved: they wore T-shirts with the arms cut off, wide blue-grey belts with big buckles that said JB, grey cutoffs in the summer and grey tightbottoms in the winter, and they always had twisted grey-blue headbands around

*203*

their foreheads. The hair was crewcut to begin with, but then they started cutting it short in the middle and letting it grow longer on the sides. When they walked down the street, they got a lot of respect, and when they walked down the street *together,* they got a *lot* of respect.

Once in a while they got into shoving matches with some other gang, but everybody knew the days of brass knuckles and auto antennas were over, and they really weren't into that anyway: it wasn't a *competitive* thing, like proving they were meaner than anybody, they just enjoyed seeing the straights get off the sidewalk to let them by, or pushing them off if they didn't. And then they would go into a bar and drink a lot of beer, and go home doing the same thing, or sometimes other things.

One afternoon five of them were walking down the street, Carter, Erv, Tim, Walker, and Mark. All in a row. And they nudged an old dentist type off the sidewalk into the gutter. Then a couple of tourists in Hawaiian shirts.

And Erv fell down, just facedown on the sidewalk, drooling on the concrete, his arms wide. And then a couple of seconds later Mark went down, just the same. The rest of them ran, but Walker went, and Carter, and only Tim got away.

That was the year when the big die-off begun. I remember it real well, because three of my relatives went that same year. My uncle Ralph, my aunt Lorraine, and my cousin Jeff. It wasn't no kind of disease—they weren't sick or nothing—it was them McNultys done it. Seemed like anybody that was just a mortal nuisance to all and sundry, why, they had better watch out, because the McNultys would get them. And after the first few months, you could see folks walking around kind of holding theirselves in, trying to be polite, don't you know. But it was too much for them mostly. Sooner or later they would take to cussing and carrying on like they used to, and that would be the end of them.

> Oral history, Paul Z. Wilson,
> recorded November 23, 2036.

This little kid, nasty little brute, about ten or eleven I'd say, red hair, freckles, mean little eyes too close together, horrid child, his parents should have drowned him at birth. He had a sort of feud going with a man named Palmer who lived two doors down. Palmer didn't like him crossing the front garden, you see. And the kid knew that Palmer had a temper. I saw the whole thing from across the road. Nice morning in May, Palmer working in his petunias. Here comes the kid on his bicycle, swerves into the garden, makes Palmer jump up and shout, goes on round the corner. Five minutes later, back again, same thing, off again. Palmer waited for him. Kid came by, riding no hands, thumbs in his ears, gave Palmer the raspberry. Palmer grabbed him off the bicycle—just what the kid was hoping for, do you see—and next moment he was lying in the gutter dead as mutton. No, not Palmer, the kid. It was a big surprise all round. Palmer quite cut up about it, but the inquest cleared him absolutely. Kid dead, not a mark on him. Cause of death, act of God—that was what they called it then.

> Oral history, Victor Levering,
> recorded February 2, 2041.

His name was Raúl Pacheco Quinones; he was thirty-five, a lawyer, a widower, a poet who never showed his verses to anyone. He thought of himself as essentially normal sexually, if perhaps a little more fastidious than most; his shyness prevented him from approaching any woman unless he felt a shared attraction . . . Well, anyhow, in his successful encounters he instinctively and naturally behaved in a caring way, solicitous of the woman and desiring her pleasure, and yet in his fantasies and in the kind of pornography he preferred, he thought obsessively of women stripped and compelled —not brutally raped, as a rule, but compelled to submit nevertheless, and moreover forced to respond against their will. And of course this was a sick fantasy, the rapist's fantasy that the victim really likes it. Later he began to have other fantasies, in which he experienced the excitement of blood and dismemberment. In actual life he would never take part in such a thing, but he remembered that as a young boy he had had daydreams of this kind, of stripping and humiliating a certain woman teacher, for example—this was early, before he had even found out what men and women did with their sexual parts. And perhaps this sadistic motif came from that time, when he had felt sexually confused, ignorant and powerless, and wanted to retaliate by injuring a woman. Sometimes, with a metal fist, he wanted to strike his parents in the face with such power that it would drive them back against their parents and grandparents and knock them all down like trees felled by a hurricane.

In a suburb of Lima called Miraflores, where he had just finished lunch with a client, he was walking down a sunny street between whitewashed walls toward the holotheaters and the bus stop, looking at the people he passed. Here a woman in her thirties, face a little drooping and sad, and he thought of closing the door, the fright in her eyes, then the first slicing blow. He saw rich rolling intestines cascading out on the floor, blood spurting between fingers, grey intestines and yellow fat, all the forbidden interior; yes, and the closed eyes, the mouth straining open to scream its disbelief. That this could happen, that another human being could . . .

He slipped out and into an elderly woman named Velásquez who was walking in the same direction. *Come and look at this, please.   Without pleasure.*

. . . another slice, and the white bone before the blood covered it; then the hairy pubis parting . . . *But he has never—?  No. He knows he would die. Unusual. Let's call a few others.*

They rode him together into a bus, where he sat looking out the dusty window awhile, then took a pad from his breast pocket and wrote:

> *Aunque me maten*
> *Por no ser feliz,*
> *Por no creer en su mundo antiséptico,*
> *Diré que el ser feliz no es lo mío.*
> *Lo mío es decir la verdad,*
> *La verdad mía, sola mi verdad,*
> *Aunque sea amarga.*

This ugliness is beautiful to him.   True. And he harms
   Then why kill him?                     no one.
      Only to spare ourselves

from having to see
these things again?
   He says his business as
a poet is to tell his own truth,
even if it is bitter.

Let him live.
What if he is unhappy?

      How can we know he is wrong?
All right. Good-bye. *Pop* *Pop* *Pop* *Pop*


Ralph W. Steinleser owned and operated an electronic parts manufacturing company in Cleveland, Ohio; he was a choleric man of fifty-six who had been disillusioned in love several times and whose doctor no longer allowed him to eat the foods he liked best. Lately he had noticed that the people in the office were giving him strange looks. The new head of his catalog department, Tom Eberhard, for instance. One morning Steinleser was saying to him, "I wouldn't wipe my *ass* on a piece of junk like that. A kid nine years old could—" There was that look again. It wasn't suppressed anger; he was used to that, and people who worked for him damn well had to suppress their anger; it was something else, almost like fear or, no, more like excitement.

"What's the matter?" he said irritably.

Eberhard moistened his lips. "Nothing."

"Come on, give for Chrissake. What are you, afraid to tell me? Come *on,* be a mentsh."

"I'm just wondering how much longer you'll be with us, Mr. Steinleser," Eberhard said.

Steinleser looked at him. "You going to explain that or what?"

"If I do, you'll fire me."

Steinleser took a grip on himself. "I won't fire you, okay? I swear on my mother's grave."

"Okay, you know Al Mahony over at Capitol Processing?"

"Know him? I knew him. He dropped dead last Wednesday."

"Right, and so did Win Colford at World, and Rich Piotto at Hi-Tek, and three or four others that I know about. Not last Wednesday, but like the last six months or so."

"And you think I might be next, huh?" Steinleser moved toward the door, turned around. "What did all those guys have in common, Eberhard? They were all sons of bitches, right, and I'm another one?"

Eberhard said nothing.

"You're *fired,*" Steinleser said. "No, the hell with it. You're not fired. Maybe I'm going to give you a raise, who knows." With an effort, he added, "Thanks."

He went back to his own office, told the computer, "Pinky, hold my calls," and leaned back in his chair with his eyes closed. Well, he *was* an SOB; he could afford to be one, and it came natural, so why not? "Pinky," he said, "there was something on the news about rudeness, when was it, last week sometime."

"Is this it?" In the holo, the head and shoulders of a local anchor appeared. "A new development in the story of McNulty's Symbiont," she said. "A wave of unexplained deaths in Eastern cities has a few scientists worried. Like earlier victims apparently killed by symbionts, they were mostly men between the ages of thirty-five and sixty, but unlike those earlier deaths, there is no evidence that they were about to commit any act of violence. They were, however, said to be extremely rude and overbearing persons, who made everyone around them miserable. In other news—"

"Yeah, that was it," Steinleser said. "Any more?"

A well-known commentator appeared in the holo. "Here's a new wrinkle," he said. "A company called Feelsafe is marketing a gadget that fits on your wrist and buzzes you if you start to lose your temper. They point to the recent wave of deaths among middle-aged men, particularly those in management positions. These people, they say, dropped dead in the middle of tantrums because the McNulty's Symbiont got them. Wear their gadget, they say, and live longer." He leaned closer in the holo, with a conspiratorial smile. "How do you like *them* apples?"

"Enough," said Steinleser. "Look up Feelsafe."

A picture came up in the holo: a computer bracelet in two styles, silver and gold, the gold one a little broader. A voice was saying, "Feelsafe looks like an ordinary wrist computer, and actually has a full spectrum of functions, but in addition it is a sensitive biofeedback device that lets you know when you are about to give vent to anger and hostility. Feel safe and live longer." The prices and order numbers were flashing.

"Enough," he said. "That's craziness." He took a cigar out of the box on his desk, looked at it and put it back. Were they killing people for being *rude,* for Chrissake? But he more than half believed it, and he told the computer to order him a bracelet, the gold model, three hundred twenty-nine ninety-five.

**27** Three Mexican-looking men were standing beside Hugh Wilkins' powder-blue BMW when he came out of the mall. "Sir," one of them said, "this is your car?"

"What's it to you?"

"It is a very nice car. Will you give it to us?"

"What are you, crazy?"

"No, we are not crazy. I think you should give us this car." The other two men advanced, one on either side. Wilkins started to back away, but now they were behind him.

"I need the car," he said. He was beginning to perspire, looking around for help. Nobody seemed to be paying any attention.

"You have two cars," the man said. He had narrow eyes, and there was a scar on his cheek; he looked dirty, like all of them.

"How do you know that?"

"You live at twenty-four hundred Live Oaks, yes? We saw the two cars."

"Well, one of them's my *wife's*. She needs a car too."

"But we have no car, and we also have wives and children."

Wilkins swallowed, turned, swung desperately at one

of the men and missed. Then he tripped somehow, and the men were holding him down while they went through his pockets. They found his keycard, took it off the ring, and tossed the rest of the cards on the concrete beside his head. In a moment he heard the doors slam. The BMW, with the three Mexicans inside, backed out of the space, turned, rolled forward and was gone.

The crazy manager at The Greentree fired one of the waiters just before the evening shift. The waiter's name was Joe Balter. "I don't care!" Limoni was yelling. "You're out, and that's it!"

Balter turned and went away, stony-faced. The other three waiters followed him into the men's room. "Hey, Joe, that's a lousy thing," Carpenter said.

"He's a maniac. See you around." Balter put his overblouse on and went toward the door.

Phillips caught his arm. "Wait a minute," he said. "Wait, wait." He beckoned to the others to come nearer. As they bent their heads together, he said, "I just had a crazy thought. Why should he fire us? How about if we fire him?"

"I don't get it. How are we going to fire him?"

"Shove him out the door and start running the place ourselves. How does that grab you?"

"Well, it would be fun," said Eckert, with a slow grin. "Hey, I'm game. You, Stan?"

"Why not?"

"You through socializing?" Limoni asked when they returned to the kitchen. Sal Aronica, the chef, was stirring something in the pot; the busboys were standing around.

The three waiters looked at each other. "Okay, Dave, that's it," said Phillips. The three of them closed in on him and pushed. Limoni shouted, "What are you doing, you crazy—!" They shoved him through the swinging door. Limoni staggered, regained his balance, and began to flail his arms around.

"Ah-ah, don't hit," said Carpenter. They grabbed his arms and kept moving, through the main dining room, past the desk where the hostess and the cashier were looking at them incredulously. One of the busboys opened the door and they pushed him out. When he came in again after a moment, they pushed him out a little harder.

"All right, listen," said Phillips, "the first thing we have to do is keep Dave from coming in again. Second thing, I'll manage tonight if you want, but then we've got to elect a new manager and revise the work schedules."

"You're going to keep on working?" a busboy asked.

"Why not? Who needs him?"

"Who's going to pay us?"

"Rita will make out the vouchers, okay? Either the front office will honor them or they won't. If they don't, hey, we'll take it out of the till. Listen, that might be a better idea. We take our share out and *then* deposit the receipts."

"You're talking about larceny here," said Rita.

"I know it. What do you want?"

"About keeping Dave out, he's got a key."

"Locksmith," said Phillips, snapping his fingers. "Harry, will you get on that?"

"Okay."

"Next, we've got to hire a couple of people, one to take

the place of whoever we elect for manager, and another to take up the workload. Rita, you want to phone the agency?"

"I hope you know what you're doing," she said, and punched the phone.

The door opened and two police officers came in, followed by Limoni. "What seems to be the problem here?" asked the larger policeman.

"Officer, this nut comes in and starts yelling," said Phillips. "So we threw him out."

"Who are you?"

"Ed Phillips, the manager."

"You!" shouted Limoni. *"I'm* the goddamn manager, and you're fired!"

*"He* was fired last week," said Phillips.

"You son of a bitch, I'll bust your ass!" Limoni yelled. His eyes were bulging; he started past the officers, but they held him back. "Just take it easy a minute," one of them said. He looked around. "Who's the manager, him or him?"

Hands pointed toward Phillips.

"Sorry to bother you," said the smaller policeman. The two of them turned Limoni around and marched him through the door. Limoni's voice had turned into a squeak.

"Why is the manager always such a prick?" Carpenter asked.

"Well, there's a theory about that," said Balter. "A guy starts out as a busboy, let's say, he does okay, so he gets promoted to waiter. He does okay as a waiter, so he gets promoted to a manager. Now he stops doing okay, the responsibility is too much for him, so he doesn't get promoted, and there he is. He's reached his level of incompetence."

"Oh-oh. That could be me too."

"No, because if you're a lousy manager we'll make you a waiter again and try somebody else."

"There's another thing, too. I went to this encounter group one time when I was working for Gentronics. I always thought these little petty tyrants got off on bossing people around, but it turns out it's really something else. They *know* they don't know enough to hold their jobs, and they're deathly afraid somebody will show them up. So they have to keep putting everybody down. It isn't power, it's fear."

"Oh-ho. All right, let me ask you this. Suppose one of you guys goofs off and I have to fire them. Then what, do you throw me out the door and start over?"

"Goofs off how?"

"Insults a customer. Screws up the orders. General pain in the ass."

"Maybe we take a vote?"

"Listen, I see a problem here. Suppose we do fire somebody, aren't they going to go straight to the police and spill the whole thing?"

"Akh. Maybe we should give this up."

"No, wait a minute. Right now, we haven't got anybody that's going to screw up that badly, so it isn't a problem. But let's swear an oath. No matter what happens, I mean, unless somebody murders somebody, we don't go to the police. One for all and all for one."

"I don't see it. The manager, never mind if it's me or not, he has to hire and fire. Otherwise you've got committee meetings all the time and nobody knows where they are. I wouldn't take the job that way, I'd go somewhere else and the hell with it. If you're right, if nobody here is going to screw up and have to get fired, okay, you're right. If you're *wrong,* then I have to fire them. If you don't like that, then you can elect a new manager. That's okay with me, but until then, I'm the manager, I manage."

"Is he turning into a prick already?"

"Maybe. Let's watch him and see."

Everybody was in a good mood that night, and they were playful and solicitous with the customers. The ambience was great; the candles on the tables had never looked so good. When the waiters went around and asked, "Everything okay?" the response they got was enthusiastic. "Listen," said Phillips to Carpenter in the kitchen, "if we keep this up, we got a gold mine."

"Sure, but whose?"

"Trust me."

The next morning Phillips wrote a net message to the home office: LIMONI RAN AMOK, TRIED TO DESTROY KITCHEN. STAFF CHOSE PHILLIPS TO TAKE OVER. PLEASE CONFIRM.

"What if they don't?" Balter asked.

"Well, fine, if they send in another manager and he's an asshole, we throw *him* out too. Listen, we can keep this up till Christmas."

President Otis took office in January, 2009. In his inaugural address he said in ringing tones, "I did not come here to preside over the dissolution of the Union. Stand tall, America!" Only about half the senators and a third of the representatives were present to hear him. Two of the major holo networks carried his address live;

one of the others was covering a solar sled race in Finland, another a nude performance of *La Bohème* live from La Scala; a third was in the middle of a marathon James Bond festival.

Harriet Owen had seen it coming. Her contacts at Peace and Justice had warned her not to expect her funding to be renewed. "Otis's people have other priorities," they said, "and besides, the money just isn't there." Hank Harmon had wept openly on the holo. "I don't even know if there's going to *be* a two hundred twentieth Congress," he said. "It's the end of the world, Harriet."

Almost a quarter of CV's support staff melted away at Honolulu. Owen gave notice of dismissal to the rest, except for a skeleton crew, and delivered the children into the custody of the Philippine Child Services Division to await pickup by their parents or other relatives. She turned over the laboratory animals to the University of Manila, and gave the department of psychology as much equipment as they were willing to take.

She said good-bye to her staff one by one. She noticed that there was a distant look in their eyes when she spoke to them; they were already thinking of where they were going next. Although they said some conventional things, it was apparent to her that leaving CV was just an incident to them, not a calamity. She took a last look at Sea Venture, lying at anchor in the harbor: the white hull was streaked and shabby; it looked obsolete already.

When she got home, she found that the storage shed in which she had left all her furniture had been burglarized. Most of her friends had left the Centers for Disease Control; those few who remained did not seem especially glad to see her. She sent out résumés to several public-sector research institutions, but nobody called her in for an interview.

When Geoffrey got home, the voices in his head had stopped. They took him to a hospital and had the implant removed, but he was still a difficult, moody child. He took a dislike to his sister Victoria, then a year old. He stole things, told lies, and was insolent to his parents. "I hate the whole world," he said.

"Why?"

"Because it's stupid."

How could we have    Impossible; we didn't
  prevented this?   know enough.    We stopped as
Yes, but it was too late              soon as we saw what
  for these few. They will    was happening.
     always yearn for the sibs
       we couldn't give them.  *Sorrow.*

**28** Caroline Bates went to work as a rigger on the Star Towers Project in 2010, when she was twenty-three. She lived weightless in the crummy for five years, with seven hundred others, mostly men. They all moved into the completed shell as soon as it began to rotate, and helped to install plumbing, wiring, and other utilities under gradually increasing gravity. She survived all this; some were not so lucky.

A good friend of hers, Larry Kleinsinger, had been working on the skeleton of Sphere A when a weld parted under tension and a structural member sliced through his leg. They heard him scream; then the sound stopped abruptly. The meds who brought in his exsanguinated body said that his helmet mike had been turned off.

The timing had been about right for him to be the father of the embryo she had aborted two weeks ago, and she couldn't get that out of her mind. It didn't make sense, because a woman could not give birth in space— the facilities didn't exist, and the contract specifically excluded it—but she wished she still had that kid. She put a message in the net to her mother, and her mother sent back: "Why are you still up there Caroline? I don't understand it, what is there for you with all that danger. Bill asks about you a lot. Come home honey I worry about you all the time." Her mother was a widow with a bad heart and a drinking problem. Bill was Caroline's ex; they had planned to go to space together, but he had flunked construction school. Neither one of them had ever been as tough as she was, she realized, in any way.

When the interior work was done in Sphere A and progressing in Sphere B, Caroline's supervisor called her in. "Bates, we're phasing out some construction people, as you know, and your name is on the list. Sorry about that, but we can offer you a permanent job here in services. The pay and benefits will be good."

"What kind of services?"

"Escort."

"You mean you want me to be a hooker? No, thanks. I don't even like this place anymore. I'll take my pay and go home."

"All right, if that's your decision." The supervisor hummed two notes at his console. "After we pay your transportation Earthside and various termination fees, you'll owe us seven hundred thousand dollars and change. Stick your thumb here and I'll have it taken out of your Earthside account."

"Wait a minute. I owe you for transportation? The contract says you send me home free any time after five years."

"You'll have to take that up with the legal department." The supervisor blanked his screen and began humming again.

She requested an appointment with Legal, and was told to go to Room 305 in Sphere B, Building 1. It was in the Services section; the name on the door was Ruby

Maxwell. Inside was a plump, dark woman in her forties. "Is this the legal department?" Caroline asked.

"No, it isn't, but sit down anyway. I understand you have some problem with your contract."

"Yes. Here's my copy. I marked the clause about free transportation."

"Uh-huh." Ms. Maxwell tapped keys, turned her screen around. "This is *their* copy. You see here, clause forty-one, where it says they *can* send you home free if they so desire. You got to realize, the longer they keep you working here, the more money they make on their investment."

"I understand that, but I've got a contract."

"Sweetie, you ain't got jack shit until they say so. What you going to do, sue the Company? Get serious. You know how many lawyers they have?"

Caroline was silent.

"Look at it another way," said Maxwell quietly. "If you tell I said this, I will call you a liar. They don't *want* to spend the money to send you home Earthside until they got all the good out of you. If they see you are not going to cooperate, it might be cheaper to space you out. It has happened before. You understand what I'm saying? You got to be nice to them, or otherwise they not going to be nice to *you.*"

They sent Caroline to charm school for a month, where she had her hair restyled, her ears pierced and her eyebrows shaped, learned makeup and perfume, got a new wardrobe to be paid for out of earnings, learned to walk and sit and hold a drink. By then the hotels in

Sphere A were already in business, although construction was still going on in B.

Then they took her to an operating room, and when she woke up she had two neat little incisions in her belly and a neat little plastic button in the top of her skull. She felt sore inside. "What did they do to me?" she asked the nurse.

"Tied off your tubes, honey."

The next day two men led her into a small room and strapped her into a chair under a black box with a dangling cord. The two men left; a technician came in, wearing an atmosphere suit. He had a vial in his gloved hand.

"Now this is just a little demonstration," he said. "You're not going to like part of it, but you'll like the other part a lot. First I'm going to show you what will happen if you screw up, and then what will happen if you don't." He opened the vial and with a glass rod put a single drop on her wrist. A pain like nothing she had ever experienced swept through her; she heard herself screaming.

Then a touch of coolness on her wrist, and the pain was gone. "That's all of that, baby," said the technician. "Now here's the good part." He brought the cord down from the machine and plugged it into her head. Bliss. Bliss. Bliss.

The memory of it was so strong that she blinked dreamily at him when he put his face close to hers. "Now listen. Can you hear me?"

"Mm-hm."

"You'll get that once a day if you behave yourself and meet your quota, understand? If you don't behave yourself, you won't get it, and if you *really* screw up, you'll get the other. So I'm sure you'll be a good girl."

"Oh, yes," she said.

She learned to retreat somewhere inside and not pay much attention. Some of her charlies were gorks, but some were friendly and fun to kid around with. If she rolled five stunts a day on her own, or eight if there were that many referrals, the rest of her time was her own. She was popular enough to get top dollar; ten percent of her fees went into her Earthside account, and although she knew they would not let her go until she lost her looks, in all probability by then she would have put away at least two million dollars; even with inflation, that would be enough to live on comfortably for the rest of her life.

Bobby Dalziel was a slender young man who worked in the recording booth when there were ballets or sports events in the docking chamber. In between, he rolled stunts for the services department. Caroline saw him with charlies a few times, and then they got to know each other. Bobby had a scheme he wanted to try out on her. They talked about it in Bobby's bedroom; the rooms where they took charlies had eyes and ears, of course, but workers' bedrooms didn't. "I don't know if it would work," he said, "but if it did, it would be enough to get us both out of here, and I want to get out." Caroline turned him down at first; then she listened. She wanted to go home, too, and it was nice to have something to dream about.

The political problems associated with the Standing Wave Transport project proved to be more daunting than the engineering ones. Nevertheless, by the spring of 2015, agreements had been signed with all the countries laying claim to Antarctica. Gravitometric and seismographic readings had found a suitable site on the high plateau within half a mile of the Pole.

A completely assembled SWT device was flown to the site in a Douglas supertransport and installed there in a prefab hut. Thereafter all materials and personnel were transferred directly to the site from Greenland, and the work went rapidly. A second and much bigger prefab building was put up next to the first one. In the second building, heat from solar collectors in Greenland was used to melt the ice down to bedrock; pumps carried the water away. More buildings were added for construction machinery, a dormitory and messhall. While construction proceeded, another site was prepared on longitude 68 W. to serve South America, then two more on longitudes 30 E. and 148 W.: these would serve Africa and Australia.

The first experimental SWT tube line, between Bogotá and New York, went into service on May 1, 2017.

**29** The idea of a weekend on Star Towers came to Harry Conlon in connection with his upcoming tenth anniversary. Harry was a large ham-fisted man who had made it big in ceramic pipe—well, not exactly *big* by Texas standards, but not so bad, either, for a guy who could barely read the sports. Jolene, his third and best-looking wife, already had enough jewels and furs to hide her completely from sight; and besides, nobody either one of them knew had ever been to Star Towers, and this would be something to talk about—a once-in-a-lifetime experience.

When he mentioned the trip casually to friends, as he found increasingly frequent occasion to do, he noticed that their eyes bugged involuntarily; that was very gratifying, and he began to think he had made an upscale decision. It turned out that Jolene had to have new jewels and furs for the trip, in order not to disgrace him in front of all those billionaires, but as Harry said, it was only money. He got a big juicy kiss for that, and Jolene did one or two things that night that she didn't usually do.

They flew to Houston, stayed in a hotel overnight, and the next morning, after indoctrination, medical check-ups and parasite screening, they put on their special

shoes and filed aboard the spacecraft with a few hundred
other people, a very select bunch, naturally:
distinguished-looking men, most of them past middle
life, and women dressed to destroy, even though they all
wore slacks or culotte dresses. "Isn't that what's-her-
name, the holo star?" Jolene whispered excitedly. "And
that one, I know I've seen his face—is he a senator or
what? Look at the *rock* his wife has on her finger!"

Harry squeezed her arm, and she squeezed back. He
figured he was going to get his money's worth just in
accelerated female gratitude and affection, but the next
part was not so great. An attendant strapped them into
reclining seats which reminded Harry unpleasantly of
dental chairs, between plastic curtains that were like the
way they curtained somebody off in the hospital when
they were about to die. Harry's heart was hitting him in
the chest; he began to feel he had made a serious
mistake.

The holos on the ceiling lit up and showed the head of
a young woman, who said, "Good morning, ladies and
gentlemen, and welcome to Hi-lift Five, Flight Nineteen
to Star Towers. My name is Wendy, I'm your chief cabin
attendant. We are now in final preflight check mode, all
systems are go, and we will lift off in approximately two
minutes. While we are waiting, I would like to point out
some of the features of your accommodations aboard.
The controls of your holos are in the left-hand armrest of
each acceleration couch, along with controls for lights
and ventilation, and the call button for the cabin attendants. The controls of the couch itself are in the right-
hand armrest, where you will also find headphones for

your holos and music, a box of tissues, and a small white envelope for your use in case you should experience stomach uneasiness in flight. Reading matter is stored in the wall cabinet at the head of every couch, and in this cabinet you will also find a mesh bag containing the loose articles and jewelry which you surrendered prior to boarding. Please use these articles with caution and do not let them escape while we are in zero gravity. Also in the wall cabinet you will find complimentary toiletries, stationery and postcards, and hairnets for use in zero gravity conditions. Once we have gone through the powered phase of our flight, cabin attendants will assist you with any difficulties you may have. As soon as the countdown begins, please make sure that your couch is in the fully extended position, that your belts are fastened, and that you are lying comfortably with your head straight, your legs slightly apart and your arms on the armrests. Thank you, and enjoy your flight."

Harry noticed that she hadn't said anything about what to do in an emergency. What did that mean, that if there was an emergency, there wasn't anything to do? After a pause, a man's voice said on the loudspeakers, "Prepare for lift-off. Cabin attendants, take your couches." Then the countdown, "five, four," and the whole thing, while Jolene was yelling, "Harry, I want to get off!" and then a roar that shook his back teeth like castanets, and a leaden weight falling over his whole body. Out of the corner of one eye he could see that Jolene's face was all pulled out of shape, like his; her mouth was stretched open sideways, exposing her teeth like a dead rat's, and her boobs were flat as cow pies.

Harry blacked out for a minute. When he came to, the roar had stopped, and now the weight was gone—all the weight. He felt like the cabin was falling, even though he knew it wasn't, and he grabbed the armrests in a death-grip.

"Well, folks," the Captain's voice was saying, "that's it for now. We'll be performing an orbital correction in about an hour. Until then, move around the cabin if you want, but please keep your feet on the floor and don't try to float around in the cabin. When you are in your seats, please keep your belts fastened."

Beside him, Jolene was throwing up. The steward came by with a little vacuum cleaner, and handed her some tissues afterward. Then it was Harry's turn, but at least he got the barf-bag over his mouth first.

That was the way it went. Even when they weren't sick, their faces were flushed and puffy, and their noses were stopped up. Harry got over the idea that he was falling after the first hour or so. But there were retching sounds from somewhere in the cabin pretty much all the time, and unless a person kept their headphones on they couldn't help being reminded, so he and Jolene didn't say more than two words to each other, and neither of them could face the idea of lunch.

They both got to the bathroom and used the vacuum toilet okay, or at least Harry did. Jolene came back from there with her face set, muttering, "I'll *never* do this again."

Then the Captain's voice said, "Folks, if you want to get a look at Star Towers, there's a telescopic view on channel thirteen now."

They turned it on, and saw a little white stick with a knob at both ends, slowly turning against blackness. A dumbbell, the brochures had called it, but if it was a dumbbell it would have to be twenty yards long. Something almost too thin to see was sticking out of both knobs, and there was another bulge in the middle. Then the view changed to the Earth, like a blue-and-white beachball. Then Star Towers again.

The Captain came down the aisle with a *frick, frick* of velcro. He was a handsome young man with a beefy jaw, and he knelt by Jolene's couch. "Feeling better, folks?"

"*I'll* be glad when I get some weight back!" said Jolene. "I never thought I'd say *that!*"

"Why, ma'am, I wouldn't say you needed to lose an ounce."

"How big is this L-Five thing, anyhow?" Harry asked.

"The arm is a little over forty-seven hundred feet long, Mr. Conlon, and the two spheres are two hundred forty feet in diameter."

"Two hundred forty? It looked a lot bigger than that in the brochures."

"Well, in fact, it really is bigger inside than outside. They don't call it L-Five, by the way."

"No, why not?"

"That was the name of the place they originally thought they were going to put the habitat—one of the Lagrangian points. Later they found out this orbit was better, but the name stuck."

"So what do you call this orbit?"

"Well, the technical term is a three-one resonant orbit, so we call it Toro. Pretty cute, huh?" He turned to

Jolene. "We'll be docking real soon, and then you'll feel better, Miz Conlon. That's a promise." He grinned and fricked away down the aisle.

"I wish he wouldn't do that," Jolene said in an undertone. "Why doesn't he stay up there and fly the plane?"

"It isn't a plane."

"Well, *you* know what I mean." She put her headphones on and channel-hopped until she found a holo she hadn't seen. Her mouth was set in a way he recognized. Christ, she had *better* feel better, or this trip would be half a megabuck down the toilet.

They watched on the holos as the white dumbbell drifted closer until it was so enormous that the ends went out of sight. They were moving toward the middle, where there was a cylindrical bulge and a cluster of antennas and things. The engines fired and stopped, fired and stopped. There was a barely perceptible jar, then a gentle rotation.

Cabin attendants rigged a guideline up the aisle and helped the passengers along it. Other guidelines led from the exit along a velcro path that curved down, then up, and eventually brought them to a big blue cylinder, like a metal cake pan sticking down from the ceiling. They got in through the open door, about fifty of them, walked up the side, and attendants velcroed their feet to the ceiling. Harry couldn't tell which way was up anymore. The attendants handed them all barf bags and got out, the door closed, and the cylinder started moving. Then there was no doubt about up and down—they were hanging from the ceiling—but after about a minute the whole cylinder seemed to swing around right-side up. A few people were retching again. After another minute the car sighed to rest; a door opened in the side. Then a glassed-in walkway, through which they could see buildings and shrubbery below, and another elevator.

The ground level was beautifully landscaped, with a lot of flowers and shrubs, but it certainly was smaller than he had expected. The brochures had made it look like a small-town park; it was really more like the lobby of a large hotel. Overhead, cantilevered sections stuck out, level after level, so that the open space was widest at the bottom and narrowest at the top. A tall window curved up one side, and Harry thought he could glimpse another set of buildings through the sunlight that was streaming in. Maybe there was another section over there, but he didn't see how that could be.

A little open-topped robot bus took them across to their hotel. The air was cool and fresh, with pine and flower scents in it. In the lobby there was a slowly rotating holo of the Earth, with numbers that showed what time it was in all the important places. A sign at the desk said: STAR TOWERS, YOUR VACATION WONDERLAND. TEMPERATURE TODAY: 72° F, 22° C. GRAVITY AT THIS LEVEL: 89% EARTH NORMAL. HAVE A HAPPY!

A computer signed them in at the desk; then a robot bellman came to conduct them to their room. Harry looked at him curiously; he had never seen one before, except once from a distance in a fancy hotel. The bellman's body was off-white plastic with inlaid brass buttons; his hands were lifelike in white gloves. His head was a holo in a tank on his shoulders. The face inside was that of a cheerful-looking young man.

Their room was on the third floor; it was sparkling clean and beautifully decorated, but pretty damn small.

When Harry handed him forty dollars, the bellman looked at it as if he had never seen money before.

"Son," Harry said, "I just got here. How much do people usually give you?"

"A hundred and up, sir," the young robot said apologetically. "Everything costs more than you're used to on Star Towers."

Harry gave him the hundred. Afterward he looked at the prices on the room-service menu, and saw that the bellman had told the honest truth. Harry had expected to be gouged, had braced himself for it, but *two hundred bucks* for a bacon and tomato sandwich?

Then he noticed a sign in the holo that said: GOOD EVENING! THIS IS SPACY, YOUR PERSONAL COMPUTER ATTENDANT. IF YOU WOULD LIKE SOME INFORMATION ABOUT STAR TOWERS, PLEASE SAY "YES."

"Okay," said Harry.

The holotube lighted up with the image of a young woman's smiling face. Behind her was a view of the sunlit buildings of Star Towers, with people strolling happily in the park below.

"Good evening, Mr. and Mrs. Conlon. Tell me, what would you like to see first—some general information about Star Towers, or the low-gravity cultural events, the casinos, the cabarets, the restaurants?" As she spoke, an animated menu appeared behind her in the tube.

"Let's see the casino," said Jolene. The computer image vanished, and they saw elegant men and women gathered around a roulette table, the men in formal evening wear, the women in long gowns. "Look at that *burnout* dress!" said Jolene reverently. "Spacy, mirror."

The holo obediently turned into a mirror, and Jolene

fussed unhappily with her hair. "I've *got* to have my hair done," she said. "Spacy, will you please make me an appointment?"

"Certainly. One moment. You're in luck, Mrs. Conlon —there has been a cancellation at two o'clock tomorrow afternoon Houston time."

They went downstairs and walked around the park awhile, looking at the other tourists, then had dinner in the hotel dining room, eight hundred bucks apiece. Jolene got a headache, and they went to bed early. The next day, after breakfast, they went to the light show and the space museum, and they watched some low-gravity ballet on the big holo in the park. There were signs all over in English, French, German, and other languages, some of them not even in regular letters. This place reminded Harry of a theme park without the rides. Except for the lower gravity and the curving wall behind the buildings, there was nothing to tell them they weren't on Earth—they couldn't even see the goddamn *stars,* except in holos that they could have watched without leaving home.

They spent some time at the pool on the top level, where the sign said GRAVITY 83% EARTH NORMAL, and Harry felt like he had lost about thirty pounds. The most desirable rooms were up here, Harry realized; that was one more thing he hadn't known when he made the reservations.

Later, looking around as they crossed the park toward a café visible on the opposite terrace, Harry saw that most of the people here looked rich but few looked happy. There were two or three younger men, flamboyantly dressed, who were smiling too broadly, probably on drugs; the rest seemed glum. A little group of Japanese went by, looking the way Japanese usually did. Then a scowling guy in a turban.

After they ordered breakfast, Harry pointed to the tall window between two buildings on the other side. "What's over there?" he asked the robot waiter. "Looks like another space as big as this one."

The waiter smiled courteously. "It's a holo, sir," he said. "Many people feel more comfortable if they can see for long distances."

Lunch, almost the cheapest thing on the menu, was four hundred dollars apiece, and dinner was seven. Counting meals, tips, and entertainment, Harry figured he would be lucky to get out of here for less than ten thousand over and above the cost of the flight and the hotel room.

That afternoon, while Jolene was at the hairdresser's, Harry went to a cocktail lounge. He sat at the bar and had a bourbon and water. "Tell me something," he said to the bartender, a tall young robot with bushy black hair. "Is there anything to *do* in this place that you couldn't do at home cheaper?"

The bartender smiled. "Sir, have you ever heard of sex in free fall?"

"Yeah. You know, I wondered about that. Is it available?"

The bartender nodded slowly. "At a price, of course."

"Oh, yeah. How much?"

"Ten thousand for half an hour's privacy in the docking area. That's if you bring your own girl."

"Girls available too?"

"Everything's available."

"Just curious—how much for the girl?"

"That depends, sir. Anywhere from three thousand to twelve or more."

"Jesus," said Harry.

Later, when he suggested to Jolene that she might like to enjoy a unique experience in space, she said, "Are you serious? After what I went through on that ship, do you think I would go into free fall again one minute sooner than I have to? Grow up, Harry."

Then she told him she was having dinner with a woman she had met at the hairdresser's. Harry grabbed a sandwich in the coffee shop and then went to the casino. He played the slots awhile, won a small pot and ended up only about two hundred down. Encouraged, he went to the blackjack table, where two men and a woman were already playing. The woman was a striking blonde in a paper dress. After a while Harry noticed that the robot dealer was paying her about two hands out of three.

Harry caught her eye and said, "Hey, if I buy you a drink, will you tell me how you do that?"

She smiled. "I just play the odds. But you can buy me a drink anyway, lover."

They cashed in and went to a booth in the casino lounge. Harry was feeling a pleasant excitement. The blonde, who said her name was Caroline, ordered a Tom Collins from the robot waitress; Harry had bourbon. "Are you a tourist, too," he asked, "or, uh—"

"I'm an employee," she said. "I was on the construction crew that built this place, and they gave us the option of staying on. The *other* option was they'd take our earnings to pay for passage home. That's the way it goes. Everybody has to have some kind of a hustle. I come over here every day or two to pick up some extra cash."

"Over here?"

"From the other half of the dumbbell. That's where most of the employees bunk. It's not as fancy as this."

"Hey, I'd like to see that."

"No, you wouldn't." She sipped her drink. "What *you'd* like to see is the docking chamber."

Harry felt himself flushing. He leaned forward. "Yeah, you're right about that. Would you be interested?"

"Sure, lover. You're heavy or you wouldn't be here, right?"

"Not that heavy. How much?"

She spread out the fingers of both hands on the table. Harry hesitated only a moment. "I haven't got it in cash," he said.

"Not to worry. I take credit cards."

"No, uh—"

"Somebody might see the statement?"

"Yeah, or— Anyway, I'll get the cash. Who do I pay for the docking whatchacallit?"

"I'll take care of that. What time are you on? Houston, probably."

"Yeah."

"Okay, late tonight would be the best."

"Two o'clock?"

She took a minicom from her purse, tapped buttons, looked at the readout. "Yes, two is okay. Go up the way you came in, take the elevator. And don't forget your velcro shoes."

Harry went to the bank and got twenty nice new

thousand-dollar bills. That night after the cabaret, taking a chance, he made a tentative move on Jolene; as he expected, she had a headache and took a sleeping pill. At half-past one, when she was snoring, he got up and dressed quietly. He found the velcro shoes in the bureau, put them in his pocket, and let himself out into the hall.

**30** In one way it was crazy, but on the other hand it would be crazier not to spend the money and get something for it, after spending so much for nothing. What if he got sick, though? He didn't think he would. He bought a pill from a dispenser in the lobby, and hoped for the best.

No one was around the elevator. He got in by himself, changed his shoes. The shoes stuck to the velcro floor, but he folded the carpet flaps over them the way the attendants had done, just to make sure.

The street shoes in his pockets made him feel funny, like a kid up to something. He realized that he was having a daydream about running into a cop named Martinez that he hadn't seen in thirty years, probably dead now. "Up," he said, and the door closed.

His weight dropped off to nothing at the midpoint; again the car seemed to roll over, and then his weight came back. After another minute the door sighed open. The velcro ramp he had come in on was gone, and now he could see just how big the chamber really was. He weighed maybe a pound or two here; his face was already feeling puffy. There she was, upside down, haloed by lights from somewhere. Beside her, a thick white rope hung from a ring on the floor. She gave him her hand to help him turn himself around and get his feet under him.

Now they were both right side up, and the big empty space was over their heads where it belonged. With part of his brain, Harry was trying to figure out why they hadn't had to do this upside-down thing when they first came in. The ramp, he realized—they must have been walking on the underside of the ramp when they came out of the shuttle, so then they were upside down to begin with, only they didn't know it. That was pretty cute.

She took the envelope he handed her, examined the bills and put them in her purse, then turned and knuckled him lightly up and down the ribs. "Here's how it works," she said. "Clothes off here, except for shoes— you'll need them later. We put our clothes in these bags."

She undressed quickly. Her breasts were small and high; when she moved, they went every which way. Harry had a painful erection. Ignoring it, she said, "Now grab the rope and just lift one foot off the floor, then the other. That's it. Now we pull ourselves up to the middle."

Harry felt himself growing lighter as they ascended. Now they were both floating, head to head, holding on to the rope. At the middle two thin cords with velcro patches at the ends were waving like snakes. Caroline caught one and fastened the velcro around her crossed ankles. "Put the other one on around your waist." Harry did it, still holding onto the rope, but he could feel himself whirling around, and he was afraid for a minute he was going to be sick.

"Let go," she said. As they floated away, she pushed herself down along his body, then swung her legs up to encircle him. She pulled herself up again, clasped him with legs and arms, and looked him in the eyes. "Now, lover," she said.

It was easier to ignore the lack of an up or down than he had expected, because the lights on both of them kept him from seeing the distant walls, but the sex itself was hard to get the hang of. It seemed like her body didn't weigh anything, because there she was floating in the air, and yet when he moved against her there was a feeling of resistance; then she would start moving away, and when he pulled her back with his hands there was a resistance again. Her boobs and her hair went this way and that way.

After a minute or two he got the rhythm better. She smiled sleepily and let go of him with her arms, laying out in the air in front of him with her hands behind her head. When he came, she drew herself close again and held him.

"Hey," he said.

"Good boy." She pulled herself in to the rope by the cord. Harry followed her, and they went hand over hand down to the bottom of the chamber.

"That was something," he said.

"Sure it was. Get your clothes on fast, or they'll hit you for another half-hour."

In the elevator, he said, "You want to have a drink?"

She shrugged. "Sure."

As they were crossing the park, they passed a young man in a silver jacket, and she made some kind of signal to him.

"Friend of yours?"

"Kind of."

They sat at a table in a dim cocktail lounge. "Listen, I want to ask you something," Harry said. "That was the only thing I done here that made any sense to me, and no hard feelings, but I wouldn't of come all this way for that. What the hell is the point?"

"Of Star Towers? The idea was to make a space *colony,* where people could live just the way they do on Earth, only better. You know, no pollution, no overcrowding, no bureaucrats. But that was a joke. Seven hundred people built this place, and it cost two trillion dollars. Figure out how much apiece we'd have to pay if we wanted to own it."

"Two billion nine," Harry said.

"Right. The project was supposed to be paid for by building solar power satellites, but that never worked, and anyhow they've got better power sources now and they don't need solar. Okay, the only other thing is a tourist trap. People come here because they can afford it and other people can't. Maybe that isn't a great reason, but that's the way it is. Sound familiar?"

"Yeah." Harry hung his head. "This trip might be the dumbest thing I've done since ought five."

"Don't feel bad. You'll get respect for it, just like the pilgrims do when they go to Mecca. I don't know what your business is, but I'll bet it will pay off."

"Yeah. You might be right. Well, thanks for everything."

"No problem." She rose. "So long, lover."

In the hotel elevator, a young man in a silver jacket got on with him. "Hi," he said pleasantly.

"You staying here too?"

"Seems that way." As the doors opened and Harry started to leave, the young man stuck out his hand. "Here's something you forgot." Harry accepted it automatically; it was a little crystic cube with an image on one side. He took one look, then barged back through the closing doors. He grabbed the young man by the shirt. "Did you *cube* that?" He turned the cube over in his fingers: one of the two linked figures had his face. The young man, looking startled and afraid, pulled away and swung at him. Harry took a tighter grip, hit the guy square in the nose and felt it crunch, but then the young man pulled something out of his pocket that gave him a pain in his chest greater than he had ever known. Fortunately, it didn't last long.

By the time the general manager heard about the killing, it was too late to do anything different. Bobby Dalziel had hidden the body in a closet while he called Caroline. Together they had smuggled it into the docking elevator, put it in a sallyport and blown it out into space.

At this point, they had at least had the sense to confide in the sexual services manager. She had bucked the problem up to the GM, Edward Goodhew, who met with his executive committee in extraordinary session at about three-thirty in the morning. The committee, which had had one or two problems of this kind in the past, authorized a substantial bribe to the purser of a departing spacecraft to accept a seventy-three-kilo consignment without putting it on the manifest, and to add Harry's name to the passenger list. The consignment was waste water in sealed carboys, just enough to compensate for Harry's missing mass. An agent in Houston would dump the carboys, and that would be that. The records would show that Harry had disappeared after he got to Houston; with luck, he would never be seen again, and his widow would never find out what happened.

The bribe came out of the contingency fund, to be replaced from the earnings of the two employees. A smaller amount was budgeted to contrive the purser's accidental death later on.

Bobby had acted hastily, and both he and Caroline would have to be disciplined, of course; but there had been no scandal, nothing to hurt the image of Star Towers. That was the important thing, after all. The committee members yawned and went back to their beds. Heigh-ho. Another day on the high frontier, another fifty million dollars.

**31** The island of Singapore, only some 387 square miles in area, was the most valuable piece of real estate on earth. There was no room for the poor except in vertical slums managed by the government. These were in the Tanglin district, discreetly concealed by a row of high-rise government office buildings windowless on the north side. By means of shore patrols, detect-and-destroy machines at harbor and airports, and frequent sweeps, the government headed by General Sun Pak had kept the island free of symbionts. Everything impossible in the rest of the world was now possible here. Murder was common. Every taste in illicit sex could be satisfied in one or more of the city's two thousand bordellos. One of the most famous was Evans' Hideaway; its slogan was "Thank Evans for Little Girls."

Here, out of cock-fighting, bareknuckle prizefighting, and Russian roulette, a new game evolved. It was described in a tourist brochure of the time:

> Game is played by two brave players in Game Circus. Player are Black and Purple, or sometime White and Red. After ceremony, each player hold revolver with one bullet to other head. Computer fire both revolver. Some-

time player are killed in first game, sometime still alive after twenty game. Player still alive after five game called Virtuous, after ten game Observant, after fifteen game Glorious and after twenty game Shining.

Another kind of Game, player are tied into holder. Body divided into twelve zones, one small charge explosive each zone. Computer chooses zone for each player, but nobody knows. Then one player or other can decide to press button and fire charges into body of self and other. If both player decide not, computer chooses zones again. No zone for vital organ. Doctor always present. When doctor says one player in danger of die, other player wins.

The player Norville Quinn wrote in his memoirs:

If you took the Big Game, or Head Game it was sometimes called, you had five chances out of six in each contest. It didn't pay much at first, but if you survived the first five, it paid a little better, and then if you were still alive after ten, a lot better, and plenty of contestants retired after fifteen, with the cash awards and the presents people gave them. If you stayed in competition, you were expected to appear once a week in the prelims, then at least once every two weeks, and once every month for champions. There were ten contests every day in the Circus, and always at least one guy died, usually two, and once in a while as many as four. The fans bet their money on who would win and who would die. The big champions dressed like princes and had attendants spraying them with perfumed oil, and they always went behind a curtain with a beautiful woman before, although it was generally known that they couldn't do anything. But they came out and strutted and puffed their chests, and the fans roared. Big money changed hands in every champion contest.

On certain holidays there were elimination contests using drugged amateurs. The contest would begin with five pairs of contestants, or sometimes seven or nine. When the first player died, the survivor of that pair would form a triad with another pair; then when the second player died, the survivor of that pair or triad would form a pair with the first survivor. With ceremonies, times out, little plays, singing and dancing, the contest would go on all day, ending when only one player was left alive. That player would be offered a place in the regular Game, but they seldom did very well.

During the first decade much attention was focused on space. The manned Martian expedition of 2004 returned safely but brought little scientific information. The unmanned Jupiter probe, which began to return data in 2007, was more successful, revealing hitherto unknown facts about the giant planet. New McMurdo Base on the Moon was established in 2010. The first space colony was completed in 2015, but the planned microwave solar energy system was plagued by accidents and failures.

Other advances in science and technology led to unexpected changes in social habits. Molecular storage and retrieval went into commercial use in 2002, making possible nanominiaturization of computers. This in turn brought about a radical reshaping of the educational system.

As a consequence of improved geriatrics and longevity

techniques, in 2007, life expectancy of male infants at birth in the United States and Western Europe rose to ninety-one years, and of females, one hundred three.

Coded stimulation of visual centers in the brain, with input from holocameras, enabled the blind to see normally. A device to monitor consciousness was developed for medical use in 2010. By the use of special lenses, it enabled the operator to see a faint pinkish glow around the head of a conscious patient. Later it was discovered by curious researchers that consciousness was shared by mammals, birds, reptiles, insects, arachnids, plants, and some stones. A new game, Chessex, combining elements of chess and checkers, swept the world in 2017. Body dyes combined with new superlight fabrics were popular in the New Sunbelt and in domed cities.

A new class of antinarcotic neurotransmitters, introduced into food and water in the remaining large cities, effectively wiped out the drug traffic in 2008. A totally effective contraceptive method for both men and women was developed in 2009. By the following year, most epidemic diseases, including all venereal disease, had been wiped out except for laboratory specimens.

Sexual intercourse as a performance art form began to gain respectability in 2012. The grand prize in the first All-Europe Tournament was awarded to a married couple from Brussels, Robert-Luc and Jeanne Dufour.

In a related development, mind-to-mind communication was made possible by computer-controlled readouts of one brain and stimulation of another. Monitoring by this means enabled the judges to be sure the reactions of tournament contestants were genuine.

A new process made it possible to recover sound

recordings from the past. Most of them were banal or incomprehensible; for instance, Napoleon was heard to say, "This is inferior shit."

In 2013, a consistent theory of synchronicity was based on the laws of chaos.

"Free systems," artificial intelligences not bound to any circuitry, were in use by 2019.

Tailored food plants requiring no care were introduced into wastelands and abandoned cities in 2020.

All this was taking place simultaneously with the social and economic changes brought about by the McNulty's Symbiont, to which we must now return. . . .

*The Twenty-first Century,*
by A. R. HOWARTH and LYNETTE FORD

A man walked into White Cloud Outfitters in Seattle and started looking over the racks of jeans at the front of the store. He was poorly dressed and wore a backpack. Grace Timmons, the manager, watched him go into the dressing room with three pairs of jeans and come out with two, which he brought to the counter.

Timmons took the card he handed her, put it into the scanner and looked at the readout. "It says here this card was canceled last June," she said. "Denver Co-op? Did they kick you out?"

"Let's say I left."

"And you haven't hooked up with anyone since?"

"No. I hurt my back."

"I'm sorry to hear it. What kind of work did you do before?"

"Construction."

"No office skills?"

"No."

"I understand the toy factory down at the end of Western Avenue is hiring. Maybe you could get a job doing light assembly."

"Look, I don't *have* to do anything." He turned to leave.

"Just a moment. You know, of course, that your picture is in the computer."

"So what? You can't put me in jail."

"No, but two or three sturdy young lads could throw you in the river. I'm not saying that would happen, but think about it. Good day."

Bubbles of memory . . . This is Kim at fifteen, when she gained all that weight. This is her mother, that same year, with her hair dyed red. Isn't that a funny hat? This is Cletus Robinson of Savannah at the age of seven. The squint was corrected by an operation the following year. This is President Otis before his heart attack. This is Emelia Switt writing the first sentence of her first novel. This is a rabbit named Bunny, the pet of Olivia Eveling of Okemos, Michigan. This is Dan Cowper out hunting with his dog. The dog's name is Bruce. They didn't catch anything that day, but the cold autumn air was great, and there was a fine sunset. This is Regina Dingwall on her eightieth birthday, surrounded by her five living children, seventeen grandchildren, and three great-grandchildren. Regina was part of the problem, but we forgive her. This is Norbert Spanbogen getting laid in New Orleans. He came down with the clap shortly afterward. This is Miss McDevitt finding something nasty in her weather shoes. This is Arpad Adjarian resigning his commission. Some of his relatives have emigrated to France, and he intends to join them. This is John Stevens working on his book of translations. His hair is white.

From the time Kim was nine or ten, Stevens had fallen into the habit of taking her with him on occasional business trips. He took her to museums and zoos, arboretums, amusement parks, restaurants; he liked to watch her when she saw new things. A complicity grew up between them. Once she asked, "Do you think people should tell the truth?"

"Always? No."

"Why not?"

"Because sometimes the truth just makes people unhappy. I try to tell you the truth, though, because I want you to trust me."

"Do you love Mama?"

"Yes, I love your mother."

"Then why do you go away with Signorina Lamberti?"

"I love your mother, but I like other women, including Signorina Lamberti. *Teufelsdreck.*"

"What does that mean?"

"Devil's dirt. It means that I am annoyed."

He knew she was unhappy at school. He had had many talks with teachers, and the trouble was not academic. "She just doesn't seem to warm up to the other children," the teachers said. Contrasting this with her evident pleasure in his own company, Stevens was secretly flattered. He thought of her as a companion, someone to whom he could be more and more open as she grew into maturity.

When she was fifteen, Kim started gaining weight. Her boyishness disappeared; she became oblong in silhouette. Julie took her frantically to one doctor after another; Kim resented the examinations and the diets which never did any good. She grew more withdrawn, even from Stevens. Her grades declined. When she was sixteen, after many conferences with Julie, Stevens took her out of school and let her study by holo. She spent most of her time in her room, or walking alone with her dog, a golden retriever who had never liked Stevens, in the woods behind their house in Ontario.

"What's going to become of her?" Julie said. "In a year or two she ought to be going out with boys, dating."

"That will come soon enough," Stevens said. He could not hide his disappointment. His bright companion was gone; in her place there was a bloated, unattractive teenager. More and more often he remembered his own bitterly unhappy childhood. "She'll grow out of it," he said.

Every now and then he saw something about Palladino in the net. There was one incident that suggested that his former employers might have taken his advice: a waiter had spilled a plate of lasagna on Palladino's head in a Berlin restaurant. Then nothing. In the holo, Palladino seemed to have put on some flesh. His skin was smooth, shining; he looked like a happy Buddha.

There had not been a reliable census anywhere in the world since the turn of the century, but some analysts, working from satellite data, had estimated that world population was down to 3.5 billion. Stress on the environment had abated somewhat during the last decade, and there were even signs that ocean biota were recovering. Atmospheric pollution was markedly better, but the damage to the ozone layer was apparently irreversible; climatic changes and flooding of coastal cities had caused much hardship.

Since the early teens, national governments had been falling apart. Quietly, without any fuss, states, provinces and prefectures stopped paying much attention to the central government. By 2020 there really wasn't any Spain, only Catalonia, Andalucía, and so on, and there was no France, only Normandy, Brittany, and the other old kingdoms. Yugoslavia and the RSFSR broke up into ethnic territories. In North America, first the southern states seceded, then the eastern, then the western. The new political units were just the old ones which had always clung to their identity, but even these could not stop the tide of dissolution. Smaller and smaller units took their place: counties, subprefectures, townships, villages. What government remained was organized by volunteers; when people saw a need for something, sometimes (not always) it got done.

Many things that had required national funding and control could not be done. Weapons stockpiles rusted in place; the orbits of the abandoned space stations decayed. Highways and bridges fell into disrepair. Harbors silted up. Airports were abandoned. It was a good thing that the SWT network now covered most of the Earth, because there was no other easy way to get around anymore.

The jails had emptied long ago and the wardens had taken up other occupations. Even local ordinances could not be enforced with any regularity, because an offender could get into a SWT capsule and be three thousand miles away in twenty-two seconds.

All the nightmares of the doom-criers were coming to pass. Respect for authority and tradition was gone; people were looking out for themselves and their families. Taxes could not be collected. Industries closed down; schools closed, churches and government offices stood empty.

According to some, hosts of unborn children were adrift through the atmosphere, keening their regret. Millions of little Anthonys and Marys, Gretchens and Borises, were lost forever. Among them were three notable musicians, two poets, seven ax murderers, six mathematicians, four actors, ten baseball players, ten presidents, and a great number of basically undistinguished people. They were not born. They did not add their bulk to the human mass. They did not send their feces into the rivers and oceans. The wind did not even whisper their names.

Stevens had foreseen the panic that came when the stock exchanges closed down, and had stockpiled as much food as he could; he had also converted his holdings into gold and precious stones, which still had a fairly stable value.

Kim left home when she was eighteen to join a commune in Kathmandu, and a year later she married a former CV inmate, Geoffrey Barlow-Geller. Stevens realized that the reason for his own marriage no longer existed, and he contemplated a separation; then Julie became gravely ill.

In 2020 her condition was diagnosed as systemic lupus erythematosus. She underwent a cloned kidney transplant at Smith Memorial Hospital in Toronto, where her recovery was slow. The medical bills came to over two million new dollars. Stevens sold all that he had.

It was out of the question for him to look for a job; there were no jobs even for younger people with work histories. In March he went to the director of the Toronto Moneyless District and asked to be accepted as a member.

"And what can you contribute, Mr. Kauffman?" she asked. "You realize that at this stage we have to worry about such things."

"I am a translator of poetry."

"And that's all?"

"I'm afraid so." Stevens stood up to leave. "Thank you for your patience."

"Wait a minute. Are you the Peter Kauffman who helped organize the first moneyless group?"

"Yes."

"Well, I don't know if your translations are any good, but we will certainly accept you. Welcome back, Mr. Kauffman."

The District didn't have much, but it was enough. Food staples were in fair supply, although there were recurrent shortages. There was plenty of housing, and the District had its own power and water. Stevens brought Julie home to the modest house they had given him and nursed her himself. There were no servants, of course, but a volunteer student came in several times a week to help him.

Stevens savored the irony: he was now completely dependent on the moneyless movement which he had once considered an aberration to be exploited, and which he had abandoned with relief ten years ago.

Intrigued, he spent part of his free time investigating the organization of the District. The membership was now more than three hundred thousand, growing by ten percent a year; it included a number of small manufacturers and suppliers, farmers, orchardists and dairy operators, construction people, doctors and nurses. Some of these were indoctrinated supporters, but the majority were people who had turned to the moneyless group because nothing else was working.

"My hospital went right down the slide," one doctor told him. "They couldn't get the capital for improvements, and the patients didn't have enough money. At least this way I can go on treating people, and I don't have to starve doing it."

Stevens kept working at his translations of Villon. They were published under a pseudonym in the spring of 2022, and had a modest success. Ecclesiasticus said, "*The Poems of François Villon,* translated by Arthur Raab, is one of the best versions I've seen. Particularly notable is his recasting of the famous Ballade of the Hanged, in several ways better than Payne or Swinburne, into which the translator, while dealing effortlessly with the formidable problems of rhyme and scansion, has even managed to introduce his own name as an acrostic —unless, dare I suspect, the 'RAAB' turned up by itself, and the author adopted it as a pseudonym in order to impress us with his powers?"

Stevens smiled.

When his doctors talked about various ailments and annoyances, they said, "That's your age," as if in becoming sixty-three he had committed some fault which, if he had been more prudent, he might have avoided.

Perhaps if he had paid more attention, the years would not have gone so fast. In his childhood a school year had been an eternity, the summer vacation inconceivably far off; when it actually came, it always seemed a miracle. Was it the boredom of childhood that made it last so long? If so, perhaps it was no favor to give children more freedom and happiness.

Sixty-three was the "grand climacteric," a term that had amused him when he first came across it. Like menopause, climacterics were critical points in a person's life, and they were all odd multiples of seven— seven, twenty-one, thirty-five, forty-nine . . . except for the last one, which, for some reason, was eighty-one. The authors of the system had not thought it necessary to go beyond that point, and no doubt they were right.

The joke was one of perspective: at twenty-one, life looked like an expanding cone; at sixty-three, seen from the other direction, it was a shape rather like a lozenge. There had never been time to do all that he wanted to do; that had been a naive illusion. He looked now at young people, with their improbably smooth complexions, and realized that they didn't know and could not be told.

He remembered that Newland had spoken about this

very subject aboard Sea Venture, at one of their last meetings before Stevens had killed him. What had Newland said? Something platitudinous and kind. After all, what else could he have said? "Seize the moment as it flies"? Stevens had always done that, but the moments had slipped away just the same.

When he was dying in the fall of 2024, the observers came and clustered in his brain, and for a moment before consciousness faded, he thought he saw them: little luminous points speaking to him without words. They were saying something he could not understand, but he thought, *It's all right.*

**32** Abraham Oberndorf, who was forty years old and had a gray-and-black beard, was a horticulturist who spent his evenings as a user interface for Hamilton Steel. The mill and shops were in the Plains, but Oberndorf and his wife lived in the Northwest Maritime, where they preferred the landscape. One evening in 2030 when Oberndorf walked into his study overlooking the McKenzie River, the computer said, "Quite a lot of calls, Abe."

"Anything urgent?"

"They're all urgent."

"On line?"

"Three."

Oberndorf sat down at his desk and sighed theatrically. "Okay, let's have the first one."

The head and shoulders of a middle-aged woman appeared in the holo. "Mr. Oberndorf, my name is Dora Wallace, I'm the supply manager of the Ringgold Design Group in Macon."

"Yes, Ms. Wallace?"

"We need a supplier for a hundred metric tons of carbon steel next year, and more later. We understand you're one of the best."

"Ms. Wallace, that's flattering, but we get requests like

this every day. All we can do is try to decide on the basis of what you tell us whether the sky will fall if you don't get the steel you want. Okay? So tell me what's so important about this project."

"Do you want a formal proposal? We're a small outfit, and we've always got metals from a jobber before."

"No, it doesn't have to be formal. Just tell me."

Wallace seemed to squirm. "Well, can this be confidential?"

"Sure."

"Okay, well, for the last seven years we've been developing and testing an all-terrain walking vehicle, and we're almost ready to go into production. Okay to give you some plans?"

"Sure."

A stack of papers thumped into the receiver. Oberndorf did not look at them. "How many units a year?"

"The first year, we hope to do five thousand. Then, depending on demand—"

"Okay, so this is basically a fun thing?"

"Yes, basically. It can go places a wheeled vehicle can't, and it doesn't degrade the environment the way wheels or tracks do."

"Hm." Oberndorf tapped a stylus on his desk. "Let me tell you the problem I see. We don't allocate any production for AT vehicles for just the reason you mentioned, they tear up the landscape. We can't stop other people from doing it, but many suppliers feel the same way, and there are a lot of local covenants, as you probably know. Well, suppose we decide to support your project. I'll take your word that your gadget causes less damage than wheels, but any vehicle causes some damage. So we might be looking at a net increase in destruction because people's resistance to these machines would be less and therefore there would be more of them out there. And also you'd be damaging parts of the terrain that wheeled vehicles can't get to."

"Actually, small sharp feet like ours are good for turf because instead of pressing it down, they break the surface and let moisture in. Remember the buffalo."

"Okay, I'm not an expert, but I see what you're saying. Have you had anybody look at it from that standpoint?"

"Yes, a couple of people. One of them is Marlene Eisenwein of Cornell. Her report is in that stack, if you want to read it. Another thing, about going places a wheeled vehicle can't—if somebody is injured, we can get to them and bring them out without using a helicopter."

"That's a good wrinkle. All right, Ms. Wallace, I'll study this material and get back to you."

Somehow the world kept turning. Young people were taught about the money society, and about wars and guns and bombs, just as they were taught about communism and the church. There was a Gun Museum in Dallas. In it could be found specimens of every major firearm ever manufactured: rifles, derringers, revolvers, automatics, machine guns; school children on tours looked at them wide-eyed. "But why did they want to kill people?" they asked, and the grownups could not explain.

Among people born after 2030, no one could remember a world in which people starved to death or were homeless or in misery. Everyone took it for granted that when they had finished their education they would find congenial work. They traveled over the whole earth, healthy and optimistic. Some liked one climate, some another. They met, fell in love, married or didn't marry; the usual size of their families was three. Year after year, the population gently declined. There was ample room, enough for everyone. The past seemed to them like a long darkness.

In the summer of 2080 one of Kim's great-grandchildren, a young woman named Mary Beth Slater, was climbing a mountain slope. Her walker's six red-painted legs dipped up and down three at a time; the feet scrabbled for purchase on the stream pebbles, put down claws; then the other three lifted, shedding bright water. Sunlight was a weight on Mary Beth's head and shoulders. The walker's body lurched back and forth just enough to keep her awake. Up the stream was the easiest route; the walker was too broad for most trails. Had to watch out for fisherfolk, though. There was one now up at the end of the next reach, a man, looked like, with waders and a funny hat, casting a white arc of line. She saw his head turn and could imagine his expression. No problem. "Left," she told the walker. It turned obediently. "Climb." It pawed at the bank, found purchase, lifted. One foot, two foots, three, up and over. Good walker. It lurched through slippery weeds, always a tripod. The streamside legs extended, the others retracted; it kept her roughly level but waved her back and forth a lot. On the whole she would rather be walking. No use thinking about that.

She passed the fisherman and raised her hand. He stared back without response. When he was out of sight, she steered the walker down into the stream again.

By dinnertime she was high in the Cascades and the evergreens were thinning. She dipped a bucket into the water, then climbed out on a meadow spangled with lupines, put her leg braces on, inflated her tent, made a fire. She was all alone in the circle made by the tips of mountains. The sky was very far away.

When the sun went down behind a peak, it was like being submerged in dark cold water. She watched the flag of the snapping flames, smelled the woodsmoke and the stew somehow not fighting each other. The first stars came out.

"Hello there!" called a male voice. It came from downslope; she couldn't see anyone. "Hello!" she called back.

Now she saw two shapes, men with backpacks, emerging from the pooled darkness. "All alone?" said the voice. She didn't reply.

When they came into the firelight, she saw they were both in their thirties, beard-stubbled and bright-eyed. "My name's Jim," said one. "This is my buddy, Chuck. We didn't expect to find nobody up here."

"Mary Beth," she said. "You like to sit down and have some stew?"

They took their backpacks off and squatted. "Don't want to rob you," said Chuck.

"I'll put some more on," she said.

Both men kept glancing at her as they ate. "Something wrong with your legs, huh," said Jim. He chewed and swallowed. "Rest of you is okay," he added.

Chuck grinned. "Sure is."

Mary Beth kept her voice neutral. "Where you guys from?"

"Newark," said Jim with his mouth full. He wiped his fingers on his red checked shirt. The nails had black crescents under them. "Good walking here. That gadget do it for you?"

"It does okay."

"Listen," said Jim, moving closer. "Is there room for two in that tent?"

"There is, but not for you."

"Don't be that way." He put his hand toward her and she blocked it.

"I'm just not interested. Go on now and get out of here, both of you."

They looked disappointed. "Serious?" asked Jim.

"Serious. No hard feelings?"

"No."

They stood up slowly and put on their packs. "Well, thanks for the stew," said Jim. As they walked away, he turned and looked back over his shoulder. "Too bad," he said. "You sure are one sweet little piece of ass."

Then they were out of the firelight, only dim bulks moving against the mountainside. She heard their voices awhile; then they were gone. She took a deep breath and relaxed; life was good. And the stars were still there.

# Appendix

Extracts from *The Moneyless Society*
and other writings and speeches
of Edgar Palladino

• What do they mean when they say I am an idealist?
They mean that my beliefs are impractical, all very well
in theory but impossible to put into practice, whereas
they are men of the world, practical men who understand how to get things done.

I prefer to call myself an optimalist, meaning that I
would like to get things done in the best way possible,
rather than to assume that the worst way is the only way.
We cannot achieve an ideal society, since we are not
angels, but we can aim for eutopia rather than for
cacotopia, the world of misery, violence and cruelty in
which we now live.

• In classical times money replaced the barter system
because it was much easier and more flexible; instead of
carrying cattle from place to place one could carry little
bits of metal (*pecunia*). The money system also led to
much simpler accounting; since everything had a money
equivalent, all transactions could be recorded in a single
category, instead of having to write down, "Fifty cattle,

five plows, ten chickens," etc. Even the USSR always used a money system, even though its currency was nonconvertible and until quite late in its history the government was almost the only employer; and why? Because of the need for accounting. And this is why people say we have to stay in the money system, because the only alternative is to go back to barter, which is too clumsy. But there is another alternative which does not involve either money or barter, neither does it involve wages, salaries, dividends, fees, or any other form of payment. It is the moneyless society, in which no one is paid for anything.

• For many centuries and in all parts of the world, the subjugation of women has been accomplished by valuing them in money. Solomon, we are told, had three hundred concubines, an exaggeration, perhaps, but he certainly had many concubines, and they were his property, valued in money just as his peacocks and camels were.

I once attended a lecture by a filmmaker who had visited a nomadic tribe in North Africa whose women are extraordinarily beautiful. In the film he showed us, we saw something extraordinary: these women walked with the men, neither exaggerating their movements for erotic reasons nor keeping their eyes down modestly, but looking about them calmly and confidently, seeing everything; in short, they behaved neither like courtesans nor virtuous women, but like free men.

Speaking of one of these women, the filmmaker said, "She would be worth a million dollars if only she were in New York, London or Paris." This was an intelligent and sensitive man, but he could think of no way to praise this free woman except to assign her a dollar value, as if she were a commodity to be traded.

In our present system women are commodities, whether they are actresses, wives, or prostitutes. But that is no surprise, because everything is a commodity. Men and children are also commodities. Under the money system everything has a value, not a human value but a market value.

When we hear of a famous man, we ask, "How much is he worth?" And if the man should be kidnapped and held for ransom, then we find out how much he is worth, or at least how much his relatives are willing to pay for him. In the money system everything is for sale, including men, women and children. And if a man or woman has a very low money value, we say he is "worthless." Yes, and we also say, "As cheap as dirt," because we do not value the soil but only its location and use. Thus, by putting a money value on everything, we are able to pervert and ignore the real value of everything. We cut down the forests because they are worth more as lumber than as living trees. We despoil the planet that nourishes us and invite our own disaster, and all because of this illusory money.

• I am asked, is there any difference between the moneyless society and a classless society? Yes, there is a difference. The moneyless society liberates us from the domination of capital with all that implies, but not from the tendency of the human race to divide itself into classes. When we look at each other we see that some of us are more talented, more able, or more wise, some more beautiful, some more graceful, and these classes will endure, but the moneyless society means that no class rules another, because all have an equal right to everything.

• I am asked, with a triumphant smirk, where will the capital come from for great enterprises? The question reveals the poverty of my critics' imaginations. Capital does not build pyramids or bridges; people build them using materials which they obtain from the earth. Capital is only one way of organizing such efforts. Long before Adam Smith was born or thought of, the pyramids of Egypt and the great public works of the Incas in Peru were built without capital.

Then my critics ask, as if they have not heard me, How will great enterprises come into being if there is no profit and therefore no incentive? They forget that in our present world many of the greatest enterprises are undertaken by governments, which make no profit; and in fact, it is often said that only governments can afford to undertake the greatest of these projects.

Even in this world, profit is not the strongest motive. A small businessman hopes to earn a profit which to him is equivalent to a living. A big businessman no longer has to worry about his living, and profits to him are no more than a way of keeping score. People build gigantic enterprises, not for profit but for glory and for love of the game. Others, such as inventors and artists, hope for a profit because they must live, but if their living were free, they would still invent or create because it is in their nature to do so.

Even if it should be true that some great enterprises would not be undertaken without the profit motive, that would not necessarily be a bad thing. Many of our greatest enterprises today are useless or harmful. Who would undertake such enterprises, except for profit or power?

• The "drug problem" does not exist; there is only a money problem. In the moneyless society, those who want to grow and cure tobacco or marijuana for themselves and their friends will do so, and those who want to make whisky and brandy will make it, and those who want to make cocaine will make that, and there will always be wine. Those who make these things because they like them and because they take pride in their work will continue to make them, but those who made them only for the money will find other things to do.

• It is said that the industrial system with its division of labor has created the highest standard of living in the world, and that even the poor own devices which even a king could not have a century ago. Yes, but these results have been accomplished by an unequal division: the joys of work to some and the pains to others. In order to buy the things we are made to want, we must labor at senseless and repugnant jobs for half our lives.

• They say that behind everything that I want to be given away lies something else that must be paid for: steel for tools, iron ore for the steel. That is true, but as our circle expands it will take in more and more of these things, and in the meantime we will manage to exist as generations did before us.

When the producers of these things ask what we will do without them, it would be better to ask what they will do without us.

• They say that some work is so unpleasant that no one would do it without being paid. Very well, if it is necessary work we will take turns to do it. Suppose we hate it so much that we discover it is unnecessary?

• They say that my system is impossible because it must necessarily involve the whole world; for example, a plow cannot be given away unless the steel is given away, and the steel cannot be given away unless the iron is given away, and the iron cannot be given away unless the ore is given away. And therefore the moneyless society cannot come into being, because in order to do so it would have to begin everywhere at once, which is impossible.

To this argument I give two answers. The first is, the argument cannot be true because it applies equally to the money society, which therefore cannot exist because in order to do so it would have had to begin everywhere at once. The second is: the argument contains a hidden fallacy, because it assumes that every end product has a separate chain of antecedents, thus the plow, the steel, the iron, the ore. But in fact these chains are linked together into a system. The moneyless society does not have to begin everywhere at once, it only has to begin in a group large enough to contain every necessary thing and every necessary skill. Yes, we must have a mine, several mines, and machinery to work the mines, and ships to transport the ore; and we must have a foundry, several foundries. And we must have physicians and nurses, and dentists, and plumbers, and carpenters, but it is not clear that we must have lawyers.

• They say that if everything is free, no one will want to work. They don't mean themselves, because they are people who would die of boredom if they could not work. Between themselves and those under them, they say, there is a vast difference. But what is this difference? On the one hand, those who labor at tasks of their own choosing; on the other, those who labor at tasks chosen for them.

• Everyone agrees that the highways and bridges need repair, and that the people who do such work are in need of employment. Why not, then, repair the highways and bridges? Because the governments concerned "can't afford it."

Hundreds of thousands of people are without proper housing and hundreds of thousands of carpenters and masons are out of work. What stands in the way of employing one group to satisfy the needs of the other? Only the illusory money system.

• Raising prices is one way of apportioning scarce goods; rationing is another. It is easy to see why rich people prefer raising prices and poor people prefer rationing.

• The moneyless society cannot at first include everyone who lives in the town, because some will not agree to join it; therefore it must be a town within a town, a map laid over a map. But since the new society will not use money except in certain emergencies, those who prefer to live in the money society will find it more convenient to go elsewhere, and thus, in course of time, the two towns will become identical and the maps will correspond point to point.

• Suppose the ten thousand people in our town have the equivalent of one thousand dollars apiece in the bank: that is ten million dollars. Since the money is not needed for personal use, it can be expended to buy things not produced by the community.

The bank, which deals in money, now operates in the moneyless community but only for dealings with the outside world. If it were still in the money system it would be bankrupt because its loans could not be collected. One or two people can operate the bank now; the ceaseless deposits and withdrawals of money have now ceased.

• The successful artist or writer will be at first a welcome source of money income to the community: but what about the many unsuccessful and aspiring artists? It is well known that nearly everybody thinks he could be a great painter, or novelist, or dramatist, if only he had the time.

Let us give everyone the chance to find out. When people discover that art is too difficult, or that their work is not appreciated, most of them will return to other occupations. Why? Because people dislike failure and boredom.

Even if we find that a great many people devote their lives to a pursuit of art which we consider unproductive, can their number possibly be greater than the number of people who now do nothing but interfere with our freedom, or add up numbers of dollars, lire, francs, yen, rubles and deutsche marks?